I0623146

PLANET LEVIATHAN

D.J. GOODMAN

SEVERED PRESS
HOBART TASMANIA

PLANET LEVIATHAN

Copyright © 2016 D.J. Goodman
Copyright © 2016 Severed Press

WWW.SEVEREDPRESS.COM

All rights reserved. No part of this book may be
reproduced or transmitted in any form or by any
electronic or mechanical means, including
photocopying, recording or by any information and
retrieval system, without the written permission of
the publisher and author, except where permitted by law.

This novel is a work of fiction. Names,
characters, places and incidents are the product of
the author's imagination, or are used fictitiously.
Any resemblance to actual events, locales or persons,
living or dead, is purely coincidental.

ISBN: 978-1-925597-01-1

All rights reserved.

1

DISCHARGED

In the glowing red light of the hold, the two guards probably thought they looked more sinister and powerful than normal. To Stacia X-79, they just looked scared. Maybe not full out petrified, but that was only because she was held firmly to the wall by magnetic locks. Both of them stood on the opposite side of the hold, likely because they had been ordered to keep as much distance from her as possible. If the magnetic locks failed somehow and they were standing right next to her, they probably believed she could crush both their heads before either knew what was happening.

That wasn't true. It was highly unlikely that she could crush more than one head at a time. The other would clearly have time to be surprised before she turned him into bloody splatter on the bulkhead.

She wasn't going to try that, though. Not only did the magnetic locks have backup power to their backups, but she had no intention of trying to escape. She had to give General Borealis what was coming to her, and she couldn't accomplish that anywhere other than where they were taking her.

Still, she flexed her muscles to see if there was any give to the locks, just in case. The locks held the hardened armor of her outer body tight, although she noticed some give where the armor fused with her muscle, skeleton, and what remained of her skin. She didn't like that. The quick hack-job surgery she'd been given to replace her Scorpio-class armor with this shoddy mess had resulted in her armor being looser than was safe. She understood their reasoning, though. The Scorpio armor was worth more than this entire ship and every person on it. There was no way they would send her to her sentence with it still attached.

But they wouldn't send her as a mostly-skinless mass of muscle and bone, either. The Galactic Marines were hardasses and cheapskates, but not cruel.

Neither of her guards was a marine, or at least not of the galactic variety. Terrestrial maybe, or possibly some other division of the armed forces. That was a curious choice. Did they think another marine might sympathize with her, possibly let her loose? Whatever the reason, that meant the two guards were mostly unfamiliar with her kind, and she could tell that they were curious.

"Well?" she asked. "I know you've got questions. It's not like I can go anywhere to avoid them."

"Quiet," the one on the right said, although he didn't sound very forceful. In fact, there might have been a little awe in his voice.

"Come on, Mahoney," the other said. "It's not like talking to her is going to give her a chance to escape."

"Hell, we don't know that," Mahoney said. "You know all the stories they tell about the Galactic Marines."

"Stories?" Stacia asked. "You act like you've never seen one before."

The as-yet unidentified guard blushed. Mahoney's skin was too dark for her to tell if he did the same, but he looked more annoyed than embarrassed.

"Regs say no talking," Mahoney said, although it sounded like even he thought that was unnecessary.

"Come on, when are we going to get another chance to talk to an actual Galactic Marine?"

"Technically, I'm not a Galactic Marine anymore," Stacia said.

"Technically, you haven't been discharged yet." The way

Mahoney said "discharged" made it seem like he thought the pun involved was rather amusing. "You know what, Briggs? I don't care. Talk to her all you want. But if she somehow convinces you to pull your weapon on me, I'm blowing your head off."

Stacia had to wonder what kind of stories the other armed forces told about her kind if they thought she could somehow make them turn on each other with just a few words. Galactic Marines were built for brute force, not psychological warfare.

Not that she didn't think she could do that, but that had more to do with her upbringing, not her training or enhanced body.

"Okay," Briggs said to her. "If you're really willing to answer questions, then why did you do it?"

"Do what?" Stacia asked, although there was only one thing he could be referring to.

"You know, what you did." He paused as though it were unthinkable to even utter the words. "Try to kill your commanding officer?"

Stacia would have shrugged if the magnetic locks weren't holding her armor and body below the neck completely rigid. "She deserved it."

"They say she had to spend thirty-six hours in surgery to remove all the bullets you put into her. What the hell could she possibly have done to deserve that?"

"That part I'll keep a secret, if you don't mind. But trust me, everything she got, she was asking for it."

"Well, I hope it was worth it," Briggs said. "Considering your punishment."

"Okay, you know what? I do have a question," Mahoney said. "They say that you Galactic Marines aren't technically human. Is that true?"

"I'm human."

"But not completely."

"I'm a cyborg, if that's what you're trying to say."

"Shit. I almost thought that part was just tall tales. So, if that's true, what happens when you leave the service?"

"Most Marines don't leave. They either die in combat or

continue on until they're enhancements eventually give out and kill them."

"But that can be almost a hundred years, at the current level of tech. You can't tell me that no one ever takes the option for an honorable discharge and goes back to civilian life."

"You've probably passed one in the streets and never even knew it."

"So you don't stay in that fancy armor? I thought the surgeries supposedly made it a part of you. Aren't you supposed to die without it?"

"Some of the surgeries are irreversible, but the armor can be exchanged. Just because we've replaced most of our skin with a hard shell doesn't mean they can't give us back something that looks and feels similar."

"Is it true ex-marines still have people following them everywhere with guns, waiting in case they still go rogue?"

"Uh, no, not completely. Ex-marines still need to be monitored. Even without the armor, they are still enhanced weapons. They don't want us getting a glitch in one of our neural implants and then ripping spines out of other civvies."

"Shit," Briggs said. "You can actually do that?"

Stacia ignored the question. "But if someone has been honorably discharged, they're generally believed to be able to handle themselves in public. No one's following them. Just case workers checking in on them."

"Do all Galactic Marines have to change their names like you did?"

"Marines don't have to change their name."

"But, our orders said your name was Stacia X-79."

"Yes."

"Wait, wait, wait. You mean to tell us that your actual, legal name that you were given at birth is Stacia X-79?"

"Yes," she said again, trying to hide any exasperation from her voice. Next would come the question of *why* she had been given that name, and even if she would refuse to answer, these two jokers would inevitably dissect the name until they realized who her parents are. No matter what she did, no matter who she shot or maimed or killed, their presence would always continue hanging over her.

Before they could ask, though, the security klaxon sounded, signaling that the ship was coming out of its light-jump. The two guards braced themselves for the ship's inevitable shudder as it stopped.

"Be alert, we are in orbit over our destination," a woman's voice said over an intercom. "Multiple targeting locks from security forces."

In any other situation, that would have been cause for alarm, but Stacia was already aware of the security protocol when it came to this particular planet. Nothing could come in or out of the system without intense scrutiny. This was just the local space-borne forces' way of saying "Hi, we see you, step out of line and your ass is grass."

Four more guards filed into the small room. While Mahoney and Briggs stayed back, their weapons now ready and trained at Stacia's head, the others carefully undid the magnetic locks that had been holding her to the wall. She would have taken this moment to stretch if she didn't think one of them might interpret that as a sign of aggression and blow her head off. Instead, she stood quiet and still while a medical doctor came in, double-checked her vitals, and declared her fit for the pod. The guards marched her across the room and down a short corridor into a hanger of sorts. There were spots for pods along the walls on both sides, but only one of the berths was occupied. The pod in question didn't look any different from the others she'd used hundreds of times before, although this one would be sending her into a situation quite different than active combat. It looked like a giant metal thorn, the sharp end pointed down at the hatch that would open up underneath it. A door was open in the front, revealing the dingy white interior of its compression couch. In most of the other pods Stacia had used, they were brand new, state of the art. This one looked several generations behind, the white interior turned a grayish brown in some parts by what was likely old sweat and vomit, maybe other body fluids if she was unlucky. There was no need to waste a new pod for this trip, after all, considering the Galactic Marines were not going to ever get this one back. Once they shot it out from the bottom of the ship, it would be lost to them forever.

Stacia sat down in the compression couch and held her arms out to the sides again so the guards could once again magnetically lock her into place. One of the guards came forward and recited what was probably a memorized script, instructing her that the locks would disengage when the pod reached the outer atmosphere that the pod would fly itself, but she would be able to access limited control in the event of an emergency. Stacia already knew from watching drops by her fellow marines that this last part was completely wrong. If something went haywire with the pod, no attempt from the occupant could save it. It would become an uncontrolled, flaming meteor blasting toward the planet below at a velocity that would likely kill the passenger even before the impact.

"Do you have any last requests?" the guard asked once he was finished with his spiel.

"Nothing that you'll be able to fulfill," Stacia said. "I have a few words for the executioner, though."

The guard frowned at the use of the word "executioner." The armed forces didn't like that term for this particular fate, whether it was more or less accurate or not. It was known that one in ten people didn't survive this initial trip. And once they were on the surface, well, most people didn't even want to consider what it was like down there.

The guards left the room, even Mahoney and Briggs, but Stacia wasn't alone for long. Half a minute after they left, Morrison came in. To be honest, Stacia wasn't even sure what rank Morrison was supposed to be, nor what branch of the service he was supposed to belong to. It didn't really matter. He had one job and one job alone, a job that no one else wanted to take, so therefore everyone else treated him with the same level of respect they'd give to a general. He walked like he had a stick up his rectum, and despite his age, the lack of lines on his face told everyone just how rarely he smiled, or even frowned. He was all business, always.

Morrison was in command of this ship. He was the executioner.

"Stacia X-79," he said, so professional that he didn't even stumble over her unusual name like everyone else always did. "You were found guilty of attempted murder of a commanding officer. Do you have anything else you wish to officially log for the record on the matter?"

"Yeah, I'm ashamed of myself."

This seemed to surprise Morrison. "Oh?"

"Uh-huh. There's no excuse for her to still be alive. I should have been a better shot."

Morrison's surprise vanished. "You know, I've lost count of how many times I've done this. There are generally three types of responses when I ask that question. The first and most common is just plain silence. The marine in question already said everything they needed to say at their court-martial. Then there's the ones like you, defiant and sometimes acting like a smart ass. There are very few of the third type, who actually act remorseful. Some of these last ones even beg for mercy."

"Shameful," Stacia said. "That kind of thing embarrasses the Galactic Marines."

"It's funny that you think begging is a worse thing to do than opening fire on a superior, but for what it's worth, I agree. Those that cry and beg probably don't last long down there. I don't usually bother offering them any advice. It would be wasted on them."

"What kind of advice could you possibly give?" Stacia asked.

"Certain higher ups are not as lacking knowledge as they like to pretend about that place. They have ways of getting information. They know the basic structure of how things work down there. And from that, I can say this: stay away from anyone else. Go off on your own. Whoever said 'hell is other people' was talking about this planet right below us."

"Why would you give me advice?" Stacia asked.

"Force of habit, mostly. Because honestly, I hope you get slaughtered down there within your first twenty minutes. General Borealis is a friend of mine. I saw what you did to her. She didn't deserve that."

"You don't know her like I do. No one does. And no one would listen."

"Whatever crap-ass reason you give to justify your actions, I don't care. She's been through enough, and this was only the icing on the cake. So I hope you are ripped apart by something or someone down there."

"I do have one last request. A message, if you will."

Morrison nodded. "Something you'd like to pass along to your mothers, I'm assuming."

Stacia felt what little actual skin she had left prickle. "No. Don't say anything to them. They have nothing to do with this."

"Who's the message for, then?"

"Borealis. You tell her, when she gets out of the hospital…" Stacia paused for effect and smiled. "That she'll get exactly what she deserves for what she did. By the end of the week, her son will be dead at my hand."

For the first time ever, she saw Morrison recoil in shock. He regained his composure quickly, though, and after a few seconds, it was as though she hadn't said anything at all.

"Are you finished?" he asked.

"Yes."

"Then let's make this official." He cleared his throat and then spoke louder, making sure that the microphones in the room picked up his every word and broadcast them throughout the ship. "Stacia X-79. It is my duty as the commander of this vessel to declare you dishonorably discharged from the Galactic Marines. As it is unsafe to allow you back into the general population, you are sentenced to life on the planet Leviathan, however short that life might be. May whatever gods you believe in have mercy on your soul."

"Do you really have to say that every time you do this?"

Stacia asked. "Sounds tedious."

"Yes. Yes it is," Morrison said.

The doors of the pod shut and hissed with an airtight seal. Then the pod dropped through a hole in the floor into a launch tube, before being shot out the bottom of the ship at a hundred miles an hour for the planet Leviathan.

2
BUMPY ROAD HOME

Stacia had approximately five to ten minutes to contemplate the direction her life had taken before the pod hit the ground, at which point either its retro thrusters would fire and slow it enough for her to survive (at least long enough to get out), or its emergency braking would fail and she would become a splatter of gore and twisted metal at the bottom of a smoking crater. Not exactly the best and easiest time to get introspective, but hey, she was used to working with what little she had.

According to the Galactic Marine Command, Leviathan was definitely, positively, one-hundred percent not a prison planet. A prison, they said, implied cells and people being locked away. Leviathan, according to them, was simply a place for them to send the people who'd been given the ability to crush skulls like aluminum cans, yet had proven themselves "unsuitable" for reintegration into society. The residents of Leviathan had the entire run of the planet. There were regular food and supply drops. It was the most humane way to deal with these people. Hell, it was a paradise, practically, a utopia.

No one with anything better than a grade school education actually believed that.

The planet, while looking perfectly fine and habitable from orbit, was prone to unpredictable earthquakes thanks to the presence of two moons in orbit, one of which wasn't exactly spherical and therefore prone to erratic flights through the sky. Beyond that particular piece of geological information, the public didn't know a lot about what life on Leviathan might be like. Nothing that went down to the planet's surface was ever supposed to come back. The exiled marines, with their augmentations, were considered to be so much of a threat that orbital gun platforms would shoot anything that came up out of the planet's atmosphere.

No matter what the brass tried to say, Leviathan was one giant cell, and the guards were trigger-happy.

The pod's inner readout started a countdown, four minutes until landfall, and with it the magnetic locks holding her in a semi-crucified pose let go. Stacia immediately stretched as much as the limited room in the drop pod would allow. The readout blinked with various threat detectors and warnings, but she ignored them. The pod would do as it was supposed to do and deliver her to the surface safely, or it would explode. Her actions wouldn't sway the odds in either direction. Instead, she prepped herself with the assumption that she would survive, and that she would immediately be in danger upon leaving the pod. Just another combat drop. She'd done them one hundred and thirty-nine times before, leaving her pod to find herself face to face with aliens, mutants, genetic monstrosities, robots, and, in one very odd and memorable incident, a cybernetic rhinoceros. This, however, would be the first time she would ever find herself up against other Galactic Marines.

You're not a Galactic Marine anymore, she reminded herself. *You lost the right to call yourself that as soon as you opened up on Borealis.* The thoughts brought back a hollow, empty feeling that had threatened to overtake and drown her for the entire trip to Leviathan. She was supposed to be a Galactic Marine. That was all she had ever wanted to be, all she had ever known since applying for early training as a teenager. Now it was gone, the one thing that had been absolutely core to her identity. Who was she supposed to be now?

I'll find out when I get down there, she thought. *Borealis, you better believe you're going to get what's coming to you.*

So. No time for feeling sorry for herself, then. Wherever she landed, she needed to be ready to come out of the pod fighting, just in case. Normally, on a combat drop, she would have her rifle and at least two side arms, not to mention a pack loaded with ammunition. For obvious reasons, they hadn't wanted her to have one when they were loading her in the pod, but she had hoped there would at least be something stashed in here with her to give her a fighting chance. The readout, however, informed her that her entire cache of weapons and supplies, stowed under her seat, consisted of a combat knife, five meals worth of emergency rations, a very basic first aid kit for those few exposed fleshy bits she still had left, and a small tool kit for armor maintenance. Not much at all, even for someone who had been trained in survival. Still, it would be enough for her to stay alive while she got the lay of the land and found the nearest settlement. Then, assuming she survived that long, she could get on with her personal mission of finding Stanton Borealis.

Two minutes remaining. Stacia rooted around under her seat until she had all her supplies ready in their rucksack. The knife she pulled out and kept ready, shoving it blade down into the cushion of her seat so that it wouldn't go flying free if the landing was less than perfect. She didn't have to worry much about accidentally slicing herself thanks to the armor, but it could always go flying and get her in the face, or even lodge its way into one of the crevices between pieces of her armor. Again, she cursed the shoddy job the surgeons had done. She wasn't the perfectly maintained killing machine anymore.

Why did I let this happen? she thought.

One minute remaining. No, she wasn't going to let this get to her. This was no different than any other combat drop.

The pod shook violently as its retro thrusters kicked in. She'd done enough drops to know there was something very wrong with the pod. The readout in front of her indicated that there must be a leak somewhere in the thrusters' fuel lines, because the fuel levels dropped faster than they should.

The pod would likely be moving slower when it got to the ground, but it wouldn't be the easy stop Stacia regularly felt. This was about to hurt. Probably a lot.

She engaged all the inertial dampeners and safety features that she could from the control panel, then braced for impact.

The pod didn't hit the surface with the force of a bomb like she had seen with some unfortunate marines in the past. But she felt the impact jar her skeleton. She probably would have bitten off the tip of her tongue is she hadn't clenched her jaw in preparation. The small space inside the pod instantly filled with airbags, deploying with a force that would have probably done more damage than the crash itself if not for her armor. It was still enough that for several seconds she felt smothered, like a giant canvas pillow had been shoved over her nose and mouth. Even through all this, she felt the pod rumble and crunch. Before the airbags blocked her view, she had a glimpse of the readouts all going dark, along with the interior lights.

Then, nothing. Several seconds of quiet.

"Open doors," she said to the pod's minimal AI computer. There was no response, not even so much as an "I cannot do that." The computer was probably completely dead.

So this is how life on Leviathan begins, she thought. *And yet something tells me this isn't even the worst thing I'll have to deal with in the next five minutes.*

Even though every single other thing in the pod had ceased working on impact, most of the air bags stayed at full inflation, threatening to smother her in the choked confines of the pod. She fumbled around in the suffocating darkness until she found where she had shoved the knife, thankfully still wedged firmly into the cushion. She grabbed it and sliced at random through the synthetic canvas surrounding her. Escaping air hissed against her face, along with something else, something that felt more foreign than the stale oxygen that had filled the airbags. Heat, coming in on a steady breeze, along with a thick odor of vegetable rot and some kind of exotic animal musk that she couldn't identify. As the airbags fell away, she saw a crack in the door seam, apparently the source of warmth and smell. Either that was the temperature and stench of Leviathan, or else she had landed on some creature that was now burning from the heated pod's impact.

Stacia maneuvered herself as well as she could within the cramped space to kick at the door. For a normal, un-augmented human, the door probably wouldn't have budged at all. For Stacia, it still remained more or less closed for five or six kicked before it started to budge and bend at the top corner. It seemed to be jammed against something from the outside. Allowing her neural implants to inject her with a small amount of synthetic adrenaline—she didn't want to use much at all, since she didn't think she would easily be able to resupply herself—she kicked several more times with both legs until one of the hinges broke. The door bent and slumped at an angle, still held up by something from the outside, but there was enough of an opening now that she could see outside.

The pod rumbled slightly, likely one of the many small tremors that periodically troubled the planet, and the door slumped a little more, allowing her to see that it was the ground itself that had jammed the door closed. Under ideal circumstances, a drop pod would hit the ground with exactly enough force to drive the thorny bottom point into the ground for stability, but not so much that the door sunk into the ground with it. Instead, the loose rock and soil went halfway up what should have been the opening. Through that top half, Stacia could see a spread of about ten to twenty feet around the pod where the soil had spread out in an impact pattern. Beyond that, the ground was covered in waist-high plants that might have been similar to grass if they weren't three times as thick and seemed to wave themselves against the wind as though slightly sentient. The air was thick and muggy and full of unidentifiable buzzing sounds, undoubtedly Leviathan's versions of crickets and locusts. Some distance beyond, there were thick, spiraling structures covered in small green polyps that opened and closed at random like mouths trying and failing to eat the air itself. The sky beyond was orange-ish in color, the sort of hue she would have assumed was a sunrise on Earth.

That was all the small opening would allow her to see for now. In terms of alien worlds, it wasn't the strangest she had ever seen. Her second ever combat drop had been onto a planet that didn't have a sun at all. The life forms that had lived there were beyond strange, to the point where, from what little she had been able to see of them, her language didn't even have the words capable of describing them.

I can work with this, Stacia thought to herself. *So far, it's nothing I can't handle.*

There was another tremor, this one slightly stronger than the last. A thought occurred to her, causing her to resume kicking at the door in an effort to make the opening wide enough for her armor-enhanced body to crawl through. Sure enough, she felt the tremor again, still stronger.

That wasn't the earthquakes. Something was coming her way. Something very, very large.

3
THE OFFICIAL LEVIATHAN WELCOMING COMMITTEE

While Stacia's enhancements allowed her to attack the door with a strength no civilian would have ever been able to muster, the drop pod doors were still intended to survey planetfalls and some levels of enemy attacks. They didn't want to budge much further than Stacia had already managed. The opening, as it was, was about as big as it was going to get. Unfortunately, Stacie still didn't think the wide shoulders of her second-hand battle armor would make it through. And during all that time, the trembling sounds came closer.

While she did as much final work as she could widening the opening, Stacia's neural implants tried to take the data they were being given and run a threat assessment. Those particular implants were designed to compile all sensory data available and create a picture in her mind of what might be coming for her, a valuable ability in the Galactic Marines when half the time they had to face something brand new they'd never seen before. Stacia had an image in her mind of the shockwaves from the things footsteps being traced back to it, then building a skeleton, a muscle structure, and skin type, as well as, thanks to some nerdy joker who had first programmed the implants, a banana next to it for scale.

Compared to the image forming in her mind, the banana was tiny.

Stacia gathered up the pack full of meager supplies and threw it through the opening, then took the knife in her teeth and started squeezing through the hole. She immediately got stuck at the shoulders. As she flexed, trying to get even the smallest amount of give, her implant finished its analysis. The thing approaching from the southwest, behind where she could currently see, was between fifty and sixty-five feet tall, with five boney legs that ended in enormous, toe-less knobs. Four of the legs were positioned like any other quadruped, while the fifth came out from behind. Its body was relatively small compared to its legs, and the simulation was somewhat unclear on what its head looked like, if it had one at all. Whether it had a mouth full of sharp teeth, however, didn't really matter at the moment. Even if it didn't look at her as food, it was still walking straight for the pod, and if any of those club-like knobs came down on the pod, she would be squashed.

Stacia registered pain as one of the loose pieces of armor on her arm caught on some of the bent metal, but as she did her best to ignore it, first one shoulder, then the other, popped free through the gap. As that was the widest part of her armor, the rest of her slipped through easily. Stacia hit the ground head first, but the fall was short enough that it didn't do any real damage. Had this been an actual combat situation, she would have been issued a helmet, but as she was no longer going to be in officially sanctioned combat ever again, the brass hadn't seen fit to give her anything more than the bare minimum to keep her from immediately dying. She rolled into a defensive position and brandished the knife in the direction of the coming creature with one hand while she secured her pack to her armor with the other.

What am I doing? she thought. *A single knife won't do me any good against that thing.* She chastised herself for that thought as soon as she had it. That was not thinking like a Galactic Marine. That was thinking like a civilian. And while she might technically no longer be able to call herself a marine, she'd be damned if she took the title of civvie so easily.

The southwest had more of those weird, organic spires, although they weren't as dense in that direction. Although they were tall, Stacia could still see the alien beast over their tops. The proportions felt all wrong to her human eyes. Its central body didn't look that much bigger than the drop pod itself, which made it look ridiculous compared to the many enormous and boney joints all up and down its legs. Her implant took in this new visual data and enhanced it for her, letting her know that yes, it did indeed have a mouth full of mandibles and teeth. And it looked to be moving right for her.

Probably the smartest thing would be for her to run. She wasn't the kind who would go charging into a fight that she had no chance of winning just because she was addicted to the heat of battle. Her mothers had taught her the value of thinking with her brain rather than with her trigger finger. But she also saw that, no matter how fast her enhanced body could move, she wouldn't be able to outrun the creature's titanic stride. She could go for the polyp-covered spires (she'd begun to think of them as trees, even though she had no proof that they were plant-based or even organic), but this thing could just walk over and around them.

So the only logical choice (if it could really be called that) was to face it. Tiny little her. With nothing but a knife.

"I'd say my chances are about fifty-fifty," she muttered to herself. Then, as she could see its nearest knobby foot clear the trees and slam down not far from her pod, she rushed it.

It occurred to her during her mad dash that maybe the thing wasn't after her at all, that it had been attracted by the sound of the crash and come to check out the pod, but would ignore her as she ran right under it. Those hopes were dashed when the thing stopped moving, and she saw the creature's fifth leg raise up and point its knobby end right at her.

Let it make the first move. Assess its attack. Learn its weakness, she thought. *This may be the biggest thing I've ever faced, but let's face it, not by much.*

An orifice opened up in the bottom of a knob and three fleshy tendrils shot out at her. They were fast, like they'd actually been fired from some sort of organic cannon, living harpoons at the end of pulsing tethers. Her enhanced reflexes allowed her to just manage to dodge all three of them, but while two of the harpoons stuck in the ground, the third twisted in mid-air behind her to whip around her waist. The tendril constricted so tight that it probably would have crushed a normal human. Her replacement armor, thankfully, wasn't so third rate that it crushed or dented under the force, but she could still register the squeezing pain.

Stacia raised her knife and prepared to make a chopping, sawing motion through the tendril, but she stopped as it retracted and pulled her up into the air. It instantly pulled her up high enough that, if she fell and turned the wrong way with her head down, the drop would kill her. Her enhancements, in that situation, should kick in and right her in the air like a cat. Her internal threat assessments, however, were telling her that the ground was the last place she wanted to be. She couldn't run from this. She couldn't hide from it. And the lower parts of its legs were covered in a heavy carapace that she doubted her knife could get through. The carapace looked to thin out the higher it got, though, until the creature's disproportionately small torso looked completely vulnerable.

That's where she needed to be. She needed to get on top of the situation, literally.

The two other tendrils yanked themselves out of the ground and retracted all the way back into the knob. The one that had her stayed out as the fifth leg swung through the air, reversing itself so that it was held up over the top of the creature like a scorpion's tale. The motion swung her through the air and took her breath away, yet not so much that she didn't see what it intended. The fifth leg was going to position her so she was directly over that garbage-disposal of a mouth and then drop her in. Her armor might have been able to resist the tendril's attempt to crush her, but she wasn't so certain that it would do the same for her versus those mandibles and arm-length teeth. Even if her armor was strong enough, her head was still exposed. Going into that mouth was a guaranteed one-way trip.

She wasn't going to let herself get that far. As the tendril swung her over the creature's body, Stacia made several hacking and sawing jabs at the flesh around her. She only managed to cut a quarter of the way through the tentacle, but apparently, this thing wasn't used to its prey fighting back like that. The tendril let go, dropping her directly over the main body. Stacia wasted no time, aiming her fall at the point where the body met one of the legs, and stabbed it as she landed. The creature made a weird, warbling screech as she pulled the knife out then thrust it in again, and again, and again. Pale blue blood sputtered all over her as she must have hit something vital. The creature whipped its fifth leg back down onto the ground to give it more support as the leg she attacked went completely limp. Even though it still had four legs on the ground, the creature's torso shifted to an unbalanced angle beneath her and threatened to drop her to the ground. Before she could fall, though, she dove at several bulbous black protuberances near its mouth that she assumed were eyes or some other kind of sensory organ. Whatever they were, they looked like its weakest point. She stabbed one, and it exploded all over her with a viscous, white jelly-like substance.

The creature didn't screech this time. Instead, it simply shuddered, its body dipping like it could no longer support itself and was trying to sit down. She popped two more of the five in all before the entire creature shuddered and gave out.

Then she was falling again. The creature's body just barely missed being impaled by one of the trees. It slid partway down the side before getting caught on one of the tree's polyps. Stacia briefly caught hold of one of the legs to break up her fall before she tumbled the rest of the way. The knife hit the ground next to her head, burying itself halfway to the hilt.

She stayed there on the ground for several seconds, assessing the damage to herself. Armor damage was negligible. No notable damage to her head beyond a few small scrapes and bruises. The implants in her head told her that she was strangely close to dehydration, but that was something she figured she could fix easily.

All in all, compared to some campaigns she had fought in, that had been easy. Easy enough that she didn't trust she was safe yet.

Sure enough, when she sat up and looked around her, she saw nine people standing a respectful distance from the creature's corpse. All of them were clad in the same shoddy battle armor as her. One of them stood behind the others, some kind of rolled-up leather parchment in his hand and his eyebrow cocked quizzically at the dead creature. The other eight all had heavy weaponry, the sort of high-powered assault rifles and cannons that were not supposed to exist on a prison world, with each gun pointed directly at her head.

The man with the leather finally tore his eyes away from the dead creature, gave Stacia a perfunctory nod, and then opened up the leather to read what was printed on it in a voice that almost sounded bored.

"On behalf of Lord Commander Alena Lexton, greetings and welcome to Leviathan. We hope you enjoy your stay and wish you a long life before someone or something horrible slaughters you. Now come with us to swear fealty or we'll blow your head off."

4
HOBBES

Stacia wasn't in the habit of taking orders from random people she didn't know, but the man had been so polite in his threat to blow up her skull that she decided it couldn't hurt to do as he said. As soon as she made it clear that she had no intention of resisting them, the eight soldiers with the guns lowered their weapons. The stoic expressions on their faces had given way to wonder and respect as they all took a moment to appreciate the massive beast they had just witnessed Stacia take down. That was sloppy of them, and it took much effort to keep her disgust of them from showing on her face. Their armor clearly marked them as former Galactic Marines, sentenced to live out the rest of their lives on the planet just like her, but they had obviously been out of the service long enough to forget their training. They should have never lowered their weapons in the face of a potential threat. And if Stacia had just proven anything, it was that, even when armed with only a single knife, she was still a threat.

I'm pretty sure I could kill all of them in under forty seconds, Stacia thought. Except for the one with the leather parchment. The way he held himself suggested he hadn't forgotten as much of his training as the others. Even though he didn't appear to have a weapon, Stacia pegged him as the biggest threat in the group if for some reason this all devolved into a battle.

She went to grab her knife, but one of the soldiers aimed her rifle again and shook her head. Stacia stopped and let the leader grab the knife first.

"All arms on Leviathan are property of Lord Commander Lexton. You will be assigned better weapons after you've sworn the oath."

Stacia had no intention of swearing to anything, yet again she came to the conclusion that it would be more advantageous to watch and wait. She wasn't entirely sure what she'd been expecting, but already she could say that this wasn't it.

"Your name, soldier?" the leader asked as she stood up.

"Stacia X-79."

"Your real name. No need to use bullshit designations anymore."

"That is my real name."

Unlike the guards on the ship, this one immediately knew what that meant. Stacia winced as he gave a low whistle.

"My, that is quite unexpected."

"You must be relatively new to the planet, if you've heard of me," Stacia said.

"A year and a half, as we measure things locally. I'm Maxwell Faust."

Stacia nodded. She actually knew that name. Roughly three years ago in Earth time, there had been quite the scandal involving a number of Galactic Marines and a significant number of vanished weaponry. Although most of the trial had been conducted in secret, Stacia's connections had at least allowed her to learn the names of many of the people involved. Faust was one of those names.

Although those involved had been convicted, rumors were that the weapons had never been recovered.

Stacia looked at the armaments around her with renewed interest.

"Mind telling me what you're doing here?" Faust asked. He must have given some subtle signal that Stacia hadn't seen, because several of the soldiers again brought up their weapons.

"Same thing as you, I'm assuming. Life sentence."

"But I know who you are. I've heard of your record. I know who your mothers are."

Stacia took several steps toward Faust, completely ignoring the weapons that tracked her and the trigger fingers that got tighter the closer she got to him. "Let's get one thing very clear. Our association may be brief or it may be long. But at no point do you ever mention my mothers again. Do you understand?"

Faust made a shrug designed to show disinterest, but Stacia could tell from the look in his eyes that he was impressed with her confidence. "Fine enough. But the point stands. The Two Who Must Not Be Named have influence. It's difficult to imagine you doing anything that would get you sent here before they were able to sweep it under the rug."

"I unloaded a whole 808 into General Borealis."

No hiding his true emotions this time. Faust made an audible choking sound. "You're lying."

"I'm not."

"Not possible."

"And yet I did it."

"No one gets the drop on Borealis."

"That's her reputation. And yet I did it."

"You're serious? You actually killed Borealis?"

"I didn't say I killed her. I said I filled her with bullets."

"You must be a terrible shot."

"I'm not. Every single bullet hit its mark."

"And she survived?"

"Trust me, no one is more pissed about that than me."

"But why? You just decided to turn around one day, forget about a lifetime of duty, and just use a commanding officer for target practice?"

"She was asking for it, after everything she did to me."

"And what exactly did she do to you?"

"None of your business."

"So what now? You've got some delusion that you can get off the planet and finish the job?"

"I know that nobody leaves Leviathan. Not for any reason. So I intend to make sure that's one hundred percent true."

He seemed confused by this for several seconds before it dawned on him. "Stanton Borealis."

"Yes."

"You can't kill the general, so you're going to kill her son?"

"Yes."

"That's cold, even for Leviathan. And trust me, you haven't even begun to see what there is to see on Leviathan."

"Does that mean you're going to try to stop me?"

"I said nothing of the sort. In fact, I'm pretty sure the Lord Commander would be more than happy to help you out. After you pledge fealty to her."

Stacia grunted something that wasn't quite agreement and yet not quite a refusal. Faust seemed to be satisfied with that. He gestured at the soldiers, who immediately took up a guarding pattern around Stacia.

"Let's go, then," Faust said, starting a march in a general easterly direction. "We actually came here to salvage your pod, but since you're alive, I suppose we should get you back to the city, first."

"You sound like you didn't expect me to live."

"It all depends on where the drop pods land. You landed right in dominatrix territory."

"Dominatrix?"

"That thing you killed."

"Why do you call those things dominatrixes?"

"Because of those whips that they can bind you with in their fifth leg."

"I take it that taking one down is uncommon?"

"No, not at all. When you have a gun. When you're only armed with the knife you're given at sentencing? Let's just say that any time we inspect a drop site in the barnacles, there aren't any people there anymore."

"The barnacles?"

Faust indicated the tree-like structures. Stacia noticed that they had taken up a path that led them right along the line between the trees and a wide-open prairie. The "grass" was abundant here, although the further away it was from the trees, the patchier it got.

"So you're not going to find a dominatrix outside of the, uh, barnacles?"

"They're the top predator among the barnacles, specially evolved as far as we can tell to live among them. Their height protects them from the side effects."

"Side effects?"

Faust stopped just long enough to indicate dominatrix blood and fluid covering her armor. "Notice anything there?"

It took Stacia several seconds to even realize what she was looking for, but when she did, some things suddenly made sense. Most of the gore was still wet from her fresh kill. In some places, however, it had dried far faster than it had any right to. And those places all happened to be where she had touched the barnacle on her way down from the corpse. The barnacles must absorb moisture. That was why she felt strangely thirsty.

"You didn't seem too concerned about walking among them," Stacia said.

"For brief periods of time, it's okay. Don't get too close to them, and avoid the denser clumps, and you can forage among the barnacles just fine. Stay too long, though, and you might as well be in a desert. If you're feeling dehydrated, we can fix that in Hobbes. After you've—"

"Sworn my fealty," Stacia said. "Yeah, I've got it."

By Stacia's best guess, it took them about an hour to reach their destination. That seemed kind of odd, considering how quickly Faust and his stooges had shown up at her drop site, but it made more sense the longer Stacia paid attention to her environment. They had probably reached her by going a straight line through the barnacles. Now, though, they followed the wandering and meandering line between the barnacles and the prairie. Although she wanted to ask why they didn't just go further out into the prairie if they wanted to avoid the barnacles and another dominatrix, she kept her mouth shut. She'd already asked more questions than she felt comfortable with. Stacia had known from the moment she'd been sentenced that it would be a horrible mistake to trust anyone on Leviathan, and Faust had already gleaned more information about Stacia than she was comfortable with. Anything she said or asked could only give him more information.

"There," Faust finally said, pointing at something slightly further out on the prairie. "Welcome to Hobbes, the capitol city of Leviathan."

The "city" didn't have any true right to that word, but it was the first sign of anything like civilization that she had seen so far. It was more like a village with all its buildings of poor construction and random size. The closer they got, the better she could see that it had been constructed mostly out of repurposed drop pod pieces, along with the occasional organic wall that looked like it had started out as the leg armor of a dominatrix.

She would have expected the soldiers to be less tense as they moved away from the barnacles, yet a hush fell over them all as they walked out onto the open prairie. They kept scanning the tufts of grass, and Faust had them pause anytime anyone heard more than the slightest rustle.

There's something out here more dangerous than the dominatrixes, Stacia thought. *Good to know.*

The soldiers relaxed again as they got to the city's edge. There was a wall surrounding all of Hobbes, but Stacia failed to notice it until she tripped over it.

"Watch your step," Faust said.

"…the hell?" Stacia asked. She looked down to get a closer inspection of the wall. It was only about ten centimeters tall, yet it very clearly ran the entire perimeter of the city. It appeared to be metal, probably also scavenged from drop pods, and was in much better repair than anything else she'd seen of the city so far. The people of Hobbes must have taken great care to keep it maintained. "Want to explain that?"

Faust waved dismissively at her. "Someone can tell you all the ins and outs of Hobbes later. There will be plenty of time once you're officially sworn in as part of the Lord Commander's army."

Stacia raised an eyebrow at that, but didn't ask anything more. Instead, as they left it behind them, she turned back to get one more look at the tiny peculiar wall. There was something about it she hadn't noticed on first glance: the grass around it. On the inner city-side, the grass grew at its leisure. On the outer prairie-side, the ground was bare, like it had been denuded by some kind of weed-killer. She filed that particular piece of information away for later.

The city of Hobbes, as far as Stacia could see right now, was abandoned. There were plenty of shacks and lean-tos peppering the landscape, a small number of larger buildings, and one or two the size of closets that Stacia suspected might be outhouses. The closer they got to the center of Hobbes, however, the more she could hear the rowdy and raucous noises coming from one building in particular. It was definitely the largest of all the structures in the city, both in length and the fact that it was the only one with two stories. This building seemed to be in better general repair than everything else around it, and the attempts to decorate it in something resembling architectural aesthetics gave her the impression that it must be the seat of government.

That made it all the more surprising when Faust opened the door onto what appeared to be a strip club.

5
SKIN TRADE

The soldiers all went in ahead of her, either eager to get out of the open of the eerily quiet streets or raring to join the festivities inside. Stacia, now forgotten by all except Faust by her side, stood outside the door for several seconds trying to make sense of this before cautiously going in.

The interior was poorly lit, so it took Stacia some time for her eyes to adjust after Faust closed the door behind her. The building, which appeared to be just a single room on this lower floor, was full almost shoulder to shoulder with former Galactic Marines in the same shoddy armor as her. That part made sense to her. What didn't make sense were the people, outnumbered by the marines about three to one, that *didn't* have armor.

"What is this?" Stacia asked Faust. She had to shout for him to hear her over the noise of the crowd.

"Pretty much what it looks like," he said as he indicated several stages set up throughout the room. On each and every one of them, a naked person danced and shimmied to the hoots and hollers of the people in the crowd. The dancers were pretty evenly distributed between men and women, with each of their audiences roughly equal in gender distribution. A butt-naked man nearby, scrawny but clean, wiggled his groin in the direction of a man and woman in armor. Both of them made a move to grab at the dancer only for them to intercept and start pushing each other. The dancer, while he had a smile on his face, didn't look like he was happy with the idea that the winner might want a piece of him.

The dancers weren't the only ones without armor, though. Although they at least got to wear ragged, poorly sewn together clothes, all the people who appeared to be on the serving staff were also missing armor, making them look small and insignificant compared to the enormous bulk of the armored former marines. Waiters and waitresses weaved in and out of the crowd with trays in their hand, and along the far wall a bar had been set up, with a bartender and ramshackle distillery behind it. There was even one woman with what was probably supposed to be a mop as she tried to clean up some customer's vomit.

There were people without armor among the customers, but they were definitely the minority. They also appeared to be divided into two distinct groups. The majority of these armor-less customers wore the same ragged clothing as the servers, and tended to huddle around tables in groups with as much distance as they could muster from everyone else. Then there were a few in much nicer, if still homemade, clothing. These didn't seem to have the same problem mixing with the former marines. In fact, judging from their places at the tables and the way the others around them seemed to hang on their every word, these particular people were actually respected.

"I don't understand," Stacia said. "This shouldn't be possible."

For several seconds, Faust didn't seem to understand, then he nodded. "I always forget that the new people to the planet have nothing but the Galactic Marines propaganda to go on. But you already strike me as being smart. Figure it out."

Stacia looked around again, but she still didn't understand. Leviathan was a prison planet, and one that was only used for former Galactic Marines. All of them needed armor. There plain and simple shouldn't have been a single person on the planet that could be classified as a normal human being.

Unless, that was, all those rumors that got passed around

among certain galactic activist groups were true. Stacia had never wanted to believe it, but here was the evidence right in front of her.

Taking her stunned silence for continued confusion, Faust explained as he led her in the direction of a staircase. "If you still don't get it, think about this: before you were sentenced, did the Galactic Marines do anything to make you infertile?"

"No."

"So you're going to get just as horny as any other person, just like you have for your whole career."

Stacia didn't agree to that, but neither did she say anything against it. Her own personal sexual desires, or rather lack of them, were her own business. She understood what he was saying, though. Galactic Marines were given armor instead of skin on most of their bodies, but there were a few places where they were left untouched, namely the genitals. The Marines didn't want to scare anyone away by taking away their ability to mate when their terms of service were up, after all.

So sex on Leviathan still happened. And where there was sex, there would inevitably be babies.

"Everyone without armor, they were born here?" Stacia asked.

"Not all of them. But don't worry about that for now. Hey, which do you prefer? Man or woman?"

"Excuse me?"

"Doesn't matter, I guess. I'll just grab one for you to sample, and if you decide they're not to your liking, you can come back down and get another one." Faust stepped away from Stacia and pointed at the young woman on the nearest stage. The woman froze, a look of absolute terror on her face, which she quickly replaced with feigned pleasure as she stepped down from the stage, trying to avoid the trash on the floor with her bare feet. The former marines around her mumbled in disappointment before moving on to another stage.

"Master Faust," the woman said with a slight curtsey. Not that Stacia was sure "woman" was the right word for her. Her age was difficult to tell, but Stacia gave it a fifty-fifty chance that she would be old enough to legally work in a place like this on any other planet. "What can I do for you?"

"We have a new recruit to the cause," Faust said, gesturing at Stacia. His words felt just as dull and practiced as the decree he had read from the leather. "You can take care of her needs while I discuss her oath of fealty with the Lord Commander."

"Yes, Master Faust," the woman said with another curtsey. She had long brown hair pulled back into ponytail and a delicate frame. She also wouldn't meet Stacia's eyes. Stacia thought that might be a blessing. Something about the young woman inspired a deep sense of shame in her that she didn't want to confront yet.

"Come on," Faust said to Stacia as he went up the stairs. The woman followed behind them, utterly silent.

At the top of the stairs, there was a long hall with several doors on either side and one at the very end. Stacia heard various moans and grunts coming from behind some of the doors. Faust went up to one, listened for a moment, then knocked to see if anyone was inside. When he was sure it was unoccupied, he opened the door, and gestured for Stacia and the woman to go on in.

"Wait here," Faust said to Stacia. "I'll discuss you with the Lord Commander first. I think she's going to have a particular interest in you. I'll be back in half an hour…" He paused, looked the woman up and down, then said, "make that forty-five minutes. I don't want to rush you. You may not have any choice in pledging your loyalty, but it's important that you realize all the perks that come along with it. As long as you keep in line, you'll find that you'll be well taken care of."

He closed the door, leaving Stacia and the woman alone.

Through habit, Stacia scanned the room for any dangers or potentials weapons. The room, however, seemed designed specifically with enhancing Galactic Marines in mind. There was a bed, a table, and two chairs made from the remains of a drop pod crash couch. Everything was stripped down to the bare essentials, giving Stacia little to work with if she needed to make an improvised weapon.

Not that she thought she would need one with this woman.

Stacia turned to her to see that the woman still kept her head down, even as she reached for the crotch of Stacia's armor.

"Wait," Stacia said, grabbing the woman's arm as gently as she could. It would be far too easy for Stacia to crush this fragile, naked woman by accident.

"Is there something wrong?" the woman asked. "Would you prefer to have someone else?" Even though she tried to hide it, it was obvious that she sincerely hoped this was the case.

"This is unnecessary," Stacia said.

"It is?" the woman asked. "Is there something new in your armor that takes care of your needs for you?"

"No, that's not... Listen, would you like to sit? I would."

"Oh. Um, okay?" The woman sat down on the bed in a way that she must have thought looked sexy. Even if Stacia was interested in that sort of thing, she doubted she would have found anything about the trembling young woman attractive at the moment.

"What's your name?" Stacia asked.

The woman blinked. "Name?"

"Yes, your name."

"Whatever you want it to be."

"No, your actual name."

"Skins don't have names."

"So I take it that's what you call yourselves? People without armor are Skins?"

"Yes. Uh, no. You're confusing me."

Usually, Stacia didn't have the patience for this sort of thing. Give her a gun and a target and she knew exactly what to do. Give her someone obviously in need of comfort, and it baffled her. Still, this entire situation made her skin crawl, no pun intended. She knew exactly what her mothers would have told her to do. Keep everyone safe who had less power than you. But they weren't here.

"Let's start again," Stacia said. "You call yourself a Skin? So what would that make me?"

"You are a Galactic Marine." It was a rote answer, like something memorized from a textbook.

"I am not a Galactic Marine. Not anymore. No one on Leviathan is."

The woman put a hand over her mouth, then moved to put the other one over Stacia's before she jerked back, realizing she had been about to touch without permission. She looked around at the walls as though she would see some spy hole that she was being watched through. Stacia had already scanned the room for any such thing and found none.

"You shouldn't say that," the woman said. "Not where anyone might hear you. Someone might think that I'm the one that said it, and then..." She didn't finish the sentence.

"They're not, though," Stacia said. "Every former marine here was tried and convicted of something that disgraced the Galactic Marine name. They lost the right to be called that, whether they admit it or not." Despite herself, Stacia heard a bit of melancholy creep into her voice. To the rest of the galaxy, that now included her, whether she had felt justified in her actions or not.

"Isn't there something that the, uh, Skins call them?" Stacia asked. "Behind their back, when the Skins don't think they can here?"

She shook her head vehemently. "No." Then she stopped, thought for a second, then turned her head away with a shy smile. "Shellheads." As far as derogatory terms went, it was pretty tame, but Stacia couldn't help but notice how the woman looked thrilled by that one tiny rebellion, and yet scared of some unknown retribution at the same time.

All those tin-foil hat activists were right all along, Stacia thought. *There really are sentient rights abuses happening on Leviathan on a scale the bureaucrats don't want others to know.*

"What are you so afraid of?" Stacia asked. "What would the Shellheads do to you if they knew you were talking like this?"

The woman's reaction was swift and startling. She practically fell getting off the bed and racing to a corner, where she pulled her knees up tight to her chest and wrapped her arms around them in what was probably the only defensive posture she knew. "Please, you can't tell anyone! I'll do anything to you that you want! Just don't say what I said!"

Stacia followed her into the corner, moving as slowly and unthreateningly as someone could in battle armor. "I won't tell anyone. I promise. Just tell me what would happen if someone decided you needed to be punished."

"You promise you won't tell that I called them Shellheads?"

"I promise."

"They would give me to an Elite."

"What's an Elite?"

"A Shellhead that's not going to be a Shellhead anymore. A Shellhead that's going to be a Skin."

Stacia puzzled over this for several seconds before the true horror of what the woman had said set in. She remembered the armorless people downstairs who had apparently held more sway than the others. That was because they weren't true Skins, not really. They were convicts like the rest of the former marines. But a marine had to have armor. There wasn't enough of their own skin left underneath to live without.

Unless they got it from somewhere, or *someone*, else.

Stacia had seen many horrible things in her time with the Galactic Marines, but this was the first time she felt like she honestly, truly needed to vomit.

6
THE WOMAN WITH HALF A FACE

At Stacia's behest, the woman pretended she had performed the intended services when Faust came back to the room. To the woman's confusion, Stacia had even made her do jumping jacks to work up a sweat. Faust came in, saw that the woman had obviously been strenuously exercised, and sent her back downstairs without a second thought. Stacia didn't need him thinking anything other than the normal sexual activity had been going on in here, and the last thing she wanted now was for anyone to think the woman wouldn't do her job and was in need of punishment. Stacia knew that she was going to return to this problem, and very soon, but for now, she had a meeting to keep.

Faust led her down the hall to the last door, then indicated that she would need to go in without him before turning and heading back downstairs. Stacia waited until he was out of sight before checking the door thoroughly for traps. Once she was satisfied, she opened it to find an office. It looked ratty and cramped by any other standards, yet on Leviathan, Stacia was sure this room would be considered the lap of luxury. There was a desk and shelves, all of them piled high with inked leather scraps like the one Faust had been carrying when he'd found her. There were two chairs in the room, as well, one on each side of the desk, and they too were upholstered in leather.

After what the woman had told her, Stacia did her best not to look at all the leather with disgust.

She was so busy contemplating how many Skins had died to make this room that Stacia didn't even take note at first of the woman sitting on the other side of the desk. That was sloppy, Stacia knew. A Galactic Marine, whether she was allowed to call herself one or not anymore, was supposed to be able to take in their whole environment in an instant. The young woman's words had upset Stacia more than she was used to, and she needed to keep a firm hold on her feelings if she was going to get what she wanted out of this meeting.

At first glance, the woman didn't appear to have a face. She was sitting with her left side to the door, and that entire half of her face was gone, replaced with a fused patch of sickly pale skin where her eye, nose, mouth, and ear should have been. The illusion was likely on purpose, a scare tactic to keep anyone new to Hobbes on their toes. Stacia didn't react. After several seconds, the woman turned, showing Stacia the other, perfectly average half of her face. She was old, probably older than any other person she'd so far seen on Leviathan, yet there was nothing about the way she carried herself that implied weakness. Now that she was standing here before this woman, Stacia remembered the name Faust had given at her crash site. It was a name she probably would have reacted to earlier, if she hadn't been so preoccupied.

This woman was infamous, after all. She was the first person to ever be sentenced to life on Leviathan.

"Hello," the woman said in a gravelly voice. Despite the fact that she was missing half her face, there was no hint of any speech impediment. "I am Lord Commander Alena Lexton."

"It's an honor," Stacia said. It really wasn't. "But you'll forgive me if I doubt that. There's no way Alena Lexton could still be alive. She would be somewhere in the vicinity of a hundred and fifty years old by now."

"My, has it been that long?" Lexton stood up from her chair and offered Stacia her hand to shake. Stacia stared at it, wondering if this was supposed to be some kind of test. After several seconds of nothing, Lexton chuckled and withdrew her hand. "Just checking." She gestured for Stacia to take a seat in the other chair, which Stacia did with some reluctance. "I do that with everyone who enters this office. Anyone who actually shakes my hand is killed immediately."

Stacia nodded. Shaking hands was an old custom, often attributed as originally being a way for someone to show the person they were meeting that they were unarmed. Whether that was the real origin of the custom or not, Galactic Marines wouldn't do it. The last thing a marine wanted anyone to think was that they were unarmed. Even if they didn't have a gun or a knife, the marine was still a weapon in and of themselves. Anyone who showed up on Leviathan and accepted an offer to shake hands obviously had never been a Galactic Marine, and if they were here it was for some reason other than to serve their sentence.

"You'll have to forgive me for not knowing the protocol in meeting you for the first time, but if you're really Lexton, then you should be dead."

"Maybe I should be, considering everything I've faced on this planet." She indicated the missing side of her face. "This happened on my first night. First contact with the local fauna. Or maybe local flora. Honestly, there aren't a lot of scientists around here to make those distinctions."

Stacia assessed the woman's armor and realized that, yes, it's make and age did imply someone who'd had it for over a century. It looked like it had been heavily modified though, with the armor plates looser around the joints. Stacia wouldn't be surprised to find that Lexton could remove her armor when she wished, with a body underneath covered in borrowed skin.

"Do you know why you've been asked to see me?" Lexton asked.

"Faust repeatedly said something about swearing fealty."

Lexton chuckled. "Well, yes. There is that. Faust can get rather enthusiastic about his loyalty to me. But that isn't the only reason. I wouldn't have asked you to my office alone if that were the case. I would have gone downstairs and had you swear your oath in front of everyone else."

Stacia nodded. "So this has something to do with Stanton Borealis?"

"Yes. Faust told me that you intend to kill him, although he was a little vague about why."

"I have some revenge I need to get on his mother."

"Still doesn't seem like a very civilized thing to do."

"So is that why you brought me here? Not only do you want my oath of loyalty, but you want me to give up the idea of going after him?"

"Oh no, not at all. You're here because, after your oath, I need to know what equipment and information you need to wipe that little shit-stain off my planet."

Stacia raised an eyebrow. "And may I ask you why you would want me to kill one of the citizens of your planet?"

"This is my planet, yes, but he's not one of my subjects. You've heard all about him, I'm sure. Does he strike you as the kind of person who would swear loyalty to me?"

"A pretentious, self-righteous piece of shit like him? No, I'd guess him more as the type trying to organize some kind of hostile takeover of your territory."

"All of Leviathan is my territory."

Stacia doubted that. Leviathan was a big planet, and Lexton was only one person, even if she was the original human inhabitant. Not that Stacia would dare say that, not when Lexton was practically offering everything she needed on a silver plate.

"But am I right?"

"Right enough. You're aware he wasn't even sentenced to Leviathan, right?"

"He couldn't be. He didn't follow in his mother's footsteps to join the Galactic Marines. My understanding is that he was never more than a low-level politician, an activist."

"Yes, and the bastard is still a politician even here. The asshole crash-lands here by accident when poking his nose where it doesn't belong, and then when he finds he can't leave any more than anyone else, he starts spreading ideas."

"What kind of ideas?"

"What does it matter to you? Ideas I don't like. Your role is not to question me. Your role is to obey. And if you do, you will be rewarded."

"Rewarded with what?" Stacia did her best to sound disinterested, as though she didn't already have a clue about what Lexton was going to say.

Lexton pointed at Stacia's armor. "We can have that removed, for one thing."

Play this carefully, Stacia thought. "Really? You can do that?" She made sure her words held equal parts disbelief and interest.

"This can be a good place for you. It has been for many before."

"And all I have to do is give you my oath that I serve you?"

"Correct."

"And you'll give me weapons and the location of Stanton Borealis."

"See for yourself," Lexton said. She stood up and went to a crate in a far corner. Stacia had noticed it in passing before, but only now did it occur to her that she was looking at an official Galactic Marines-issue heavy weapons crate. Lexton opened a latch to show Stacia the contents: two 808 heavy assault rifles, four Arliss-Mercer plasma pistols, multiple magazines for all six weapons, and two sonic blades that made the knife she'd come here with look like a butter knife. In other words, a standard armament package for Galactic Marines readying for an assault.

Jackpot, she thought. *Probably courtesy of Mr. Faust.*

She whistled, pretending to be surprised at the crate's contents. "How did you get this?"

"It doesn't matter." Lexton went back to her desk and rummaged around for a particular piece of leather. "Here are the coordinates of where my people believe Borealis to be."

"If you know where he is, why wait for me to come along? Why haven't you already sent someone to take him out?"

"It needs to look like I wasn't involved. I don't want him to come off as a martyr for his beliefs. If you do it, considering you already have a compelling reason, it won't necessarily be connected immediately to me."

"Even though everyone downstairs already say me come up to swear my oath?"

"It's not the people here you need to convince. It's the people Borealis has surrounded himself with. Again, it is not your place to ask questions. You either accept or you don't." Lexton picked up one of the plasma pistols and aimed it at Stacia's head.

"And I assume that's what happens if I don't?"

"Of course."

"All that sounds like something I can live with. But there's one other thing I want before I say yes."

"That's ballsy of you, Miss X-79. You aren't exactly in a position to bargain."

"Given what I've seen so far, and considering that you want me to go further than any of your other recruits, I don't personally think what I want is too much to ask for."

"And that would be?"

"The woman I was with before I came in here. I want her."

"Didn't you already have her?"

"I want her permanently. I want to take her with me."

"Really? Do you honestly think I'll just give you another human being?"

"From what I've seen so far? Yes."

"Ha! Very well. I think maybe I can let this happen just this once."

"I would like her here now, to ensure she's part of the deal. I don't want anyone else doing something with her in the meantime."

"Fair enough." Lexton went to open the door, where she found Faust waiting patiently on the other side. "Faust, go get whatever Skin Stacia was playing with earlier."

Faust looked surprised. "Already? Should I have Quince prepare his saws and scalpels?"

Stacia had to fight not to turn green at that comment.

"No, no, not yet. She just wanted a little something extra to play with while she does her job."

Faust shrugged. "I'll be right back with her."

Stacia stayed sitting in her seat as Lexton went back to her own. "So what do I have to do for this oath?" Stacia asked.

"Simple. Just raise your right hand and say, 'I swear my allegiance to the Lord Commander Lexton."

"Wait, that's it? No blood ceremony, no bomb in my neck in case I betray you?"

"If you betray me, I kill you, that simple. And I don't send any of my people to do the job. I do it myself, in as public a fashion as possible. Someone tries something every so often, and once I'm finished with them, everyone else gets the hint. Effective and uncomplicated at the same time. So do you swear?"

Stacia heard two pairs of footsteps coming down the hall from behind her, one the heavy step of someone in armor, and the other the barely perceptible patter of someone barefoot and trying not to give anyone around her a reason to be angry. Stacia dropped her left hand out of Lexton's sight while raising her right. "I swear my allegiance to Lord Commander Lexton."

"Good." Lexton set her plasma pistol on the desk, making sure to still keep it within easy reach. "It would probably be best if as few people see you go as possible."

Stacia stood up and inspected the remaining contents of the crate. Although she had her back to the rest of the room, she kept very close track of the sounds. Lexton didn't immediately reach for her gun, but neither did she relax her posture. In Stacia's opinion, the woman had gotten extremely rusty, given the century plus she'd been away from the Galactic Marines and what looked like the complacency of unchallenged power. But she wasn't a complete idiot, either. She knew that if Stacia was going to do something stupid, it would be now.

Stacia picked up and pretended to inspect a pistol, as though she didn't already know exactly what it was and what it was capable of.

Surreptitiously, Stacia clicked off the safety.

My mamas always did tell me I could stand to use a few more brain cells, she thought.

The twin footsteps ceased just inside the door. It sounded like the Skin was just inside the threshold while Faust was outside. Kind of a dumb tactical choice for him. The Shellheads on this planet really had forgotten where they came from.

"It's going to be kind of hard to get out unseen with all the people downstairs. Do you have another way out?"

"No. Not unless you count the chute I use for the dead bodies." There was a clicking noise from behind Stacia as Lexton grabbed her gun. "By the way, I know you think you were being cute, but it really was a dumb move."

"What?" Stacia asked, not daring to move. "I don't…"

"You hid your other hand. While you were swearing."

"So? That's not…"

"You had your fingers crossed."

All four people stood in absolute silence for half a second.

Then there was chaos.

7
BARROOM BLITZ

Stacia realized almost too late that there was no way Lexton would leave the other plasma pistols primed with a full charge when she had any doubt at all as to someone's loyalty. Had this not occurred to her, Stacia might have wasted time trying to shoot Lexton and getting nothing but a face full of burning hot plasma for her efforts. Instead, as she spun around to face Lexton, she used the pistol in her hand as a hammer, smashing it into the blank side of Lexton's face. Lexton's intended killshot went to the side, burning through a stack of leather sheets. Stacia's neural implants went hot, instantly assessing the situation, and telling her that she had been wrong about her assumptions regarding Faust. He hadn't put himself in a bad place at all. Instead, with the doorframe around him and the Skin in front of him as a human shield, Faust had her at a distinct disadvantage. Fortunately for Stacia, he was also armed with the wrong kind of weapon for close quarters combat. He tried to aim his heavy 808 at Stacia, but it was too bulky for him to get a good shot around the Skin.

Stacia took advantage of that awkward moment to make another swing at Lexton, this time trying to batter the pistol out of her hand. It worked, and the gun hit the floor and skidded beneath the desk. Stacia had hoped it would be where she could easily grab it, but at least for the moment, it wasn't where Lexton could quickly get it either. Realizing the guns in the crate were practically useless to her at the moment, Stacia grabbed one of the sonic blades, activated the trigger in its hilt, and took a swipe at Lexton. Whatever implants Lexton was running in her head would be horribly out of date, but they still allowed her to duck and roll backward to avoid Stacia's attack.

She heard the naked woman scream right as Stacia's implants told her Faust was about to become a bigger danger. Unlike Lexton, Faust's implants would be almost as up to date as Stacia's, meaning his threat assessment and strategic ability would be almost as quick. Stacia looked to see that Faust has tossed his gun to the side just outside the door and pulled his own sonic blade, which he was raising to the woman's neck. Stacia didn't wait to see if this was intended as a threat to get her to stand down or if Faust really was going to kill the woman. Stacia threw her blade. The vibrating mechanism that allowed it to slice through steel like lard didn't work when it wasn't in someone's actual hand, but Stacia's aim was true enough for it to just barely missed the woman's shoulder and embed in the gap between armor plates at Faust's elbow. He hissed and dropped his own knife, then shoved the woman at Stacia as a distraction. Stacia caught the woman from falling even as she grabbed the next sonic blade and prepared to use it on Lexton.

Lexton was already running out the door, however, and both she and Faust disappeared from sight. Stacia took a defensive stance at the doorframe and looked around the corner to see them disappear into one of the rooms on the side, slamming the door shut behind them.

"Where's that door lead?" Stacia said in a hissing whisper to the Skin.

"Wha... what?" the woman asked, still clutching at Stacia's arm for support. "I don't..."

"That door! Where does it go?"

"Um, another bedroom?"

"Why would they lock themselves in a bedroom?"

"That's the bedroom none of us like to use. It has a window

with blood dried all around it."

That would make it the other exit that Lexton had mentioned. It also made that an unlikely way for Stacia and the woman to escape themselves. Faust and Lexton could be waiting outside on the ground, preparing for an ambush.

"Are there any other bedrooms with windows?" Stacia asked.

"N…no. They don't want us to be able to escape."

Stacia nodded as she hurriedly went back to the crate and started loading the weapons. No other way off the second floor meant they would have to use the stairs and go back through the club or bar or whatever it was. Right through the room packed with armored ex-marines.

"I don't understand," the woman said. "What's happening?"

"I wasn't a fan of the so-called Lord Commander. I didn't feel like taking orders from her."

"But everyone takes orders from her."

"Not me."

Stacia inserted charge packs into each of the pistols. They wouldn't be ready to fire for at least fifteen minutes, but until then, she had the 808s, the sonic blade, and there was still the pistol under the desk. She grabbed all the extra ammunition she could and shoved it into her survival sack, then turned to look at the Skin again. The woman stood completely rigid, her eyes tightly shut.

"What are you doing?" Stacia asked.

"Please. Just make it quick."

"Excuse me?"

The woman opened one eye. "Aren't you going to kill me?"

"Why would I kill you?"

The woman's mouth worked for a second as though that question were so bizarre that she couldn't come up with an answer.

"I had Faust bring you up here so I could take you with me."

The woman's muscles un-tensed. "Oh. Oh yes, of course."

"Do you know how to use any of these?" Stacia asked, indicating the weapons, then realized that was a stupid question. "No, of course not. I'm betting you've never even been allowed to so much as touch one."

"You… you want me to use a weapon?"

"Here, take this," Stacia said, handing the woman her sonic blade. "If you hold it just like *this*, it'll vibrate and cut through practically anything. Keep the blade well away from your skin."

The woman held the knife as far away as her arm would stretch.

"Uh, good enough. Just swing it at anyone that comes at you. I don't suppose you have any clothes on this floor that you can put on up here?"

The woman stared at her.

"I guess not. Are you ready?"

"I still don't even understand what's going on."

"Just keep close to me. I'll protect you."

"From what?"

"If we're lucky, nothing. But I'm pretty sure we're not lucky."

Stacia gestured for the Skin to be quite as they crept down the hall. If anyone on any other planet saw them, she was sure they would look absurd: a woman in full battle armor with six different guns strapped to her trying to sneak down the upstairs hall in a bar followed by a butt-naked woman holding a knife straight out in front of her. But here on Leviathan, she was hoping that anyone that saw them wouldn't look twice, or at the very least would be drunk enough that if they did look twice, Stacia could drop them before they could sound any alarm. They got back to the end of the hallway without incident, although the sounds coming from behind two of the doors told Stacia that they weren't completely alone on the floor. She would have to watch their six if something went wrong.

As soon as Stacia took two steps down the stairs, something did indeed go wrong.

"Everyone!" someone screamed from downstairs. Faust. "This is not a drill! Oathbreaker upstairs!"

All sounds from below stopped. Stacia stopped too, wondering if it was maybe too late to go back and try their luck with the window. But that would be just as problematic as earlier. Faust might have come around to the main entrance of the building, but Lexton would still be waiting below. She might even not be alone anymore.

Potential ambush behind me, definite ambush ahead, Stacia thought, then smiled. *Actually, ahead sounds a lot more fun.*

She put a hand on the Skin's shoulder for a moment, hoping she would get that she should stay put. Then Stacia unslung one of the 808s from her back and jumped headfirst down the rest of the stairs.

It was an unbelievably stupid move, which thankfully meant that no one could have possibly thought to prepare for it. Before she was even halfway down, she fired multiple rounds blindly into the ceiling, hoping that would be enough to distract a number of the patrons. Stacia's implants registered that it did, although not as many as she had hoped and not the right ones. The Skins in the room, apparently ready for everything to explode into violence at a moment's notice, nearly all ducked and a covered. A few of the ex-marines, likely some of the drunker ones judging by their proximity to the bar, followed suit. From what remained, Stacia scanned the room and registered sixty-four people remaining on their feet, fifty-eight of them in the early stages of taking a hostile position.

Fifty-eight targets, all of them as highly trained as me, Stacia thought. *Let's see if I can do this in under five minutes.*

Before Stacia even hit the floor, she'd blown two heads off.

She did the sideways tuck and roll when she landed that she'd been trained to do when she was carrying so much gear. The threat assessment went from fifty-six to fifty-nine as three more people decided it was better to fight than run. Making sure her 808 was set to short bursts rather than continuous fire, Stacia swung the weapon around and made headshots at the eight nearest Shellheads. The bullets connected dead on with four and grazed two. In any other circumstances, Stacia would have been horrified that she'd missed at all, but by now, every person in the room with implants should be running their own threat assessments. The element of surprise was disappearing quickly.

One of the Shellheads she'd missed ducked low behind one of

the stages, while the other pulled out a sonic knife and did a pirouetting lunge at Stacia. She recognized this one as Derre Mur, a woman who had been discharged for pit-fighting. Although that alone was not considered a dischargeable offense, since Galactic Marines making money on the side as pit-fighters was kind of an open secret that the bureaucrats tried to hide under the rug, this woman had been known for taking particular glee in killing her opponents. She wasn't the kind of person Stacia wanted to take on in a melee.

From some far spot in the back of the room, some man drunkenly screamed, "Everyone attack!" This was promptly followed by a spray of bullets that hit more of the person's erstwhile friends instead of Stacia. This provided Stacia the perfect opportunity to duck out of the way of Mur's attacks, and she dashed over to a Skin cowering nearby to shove her down before a stray bullet got her. The Shellheads might be able to survive a body shot just fine, but Stacia doubted Leviathan had the medical supplies to help a randomly injured Skin.

In Stacia's mind, the red of many of the direct threats to her turned to a burning orange as the stray bullets caused many to turn on the nearest person and take out whatever aggressions they'd pent up. Faust might have intended to get everyone in the bar to go after Stacia, but all he'd done was start a barroom brawl. Stacia scanned the immediate area for anymore Skins in danger, found that most of them were sufficiently out of the way, and then took advantage of the chaos to run back to the stairs. She had to duck one drunken punch and redirect one not-so-drunken kick into someone else, but otherwise made it with minimal effort. She looked up to see the Skin staring down at her with a wide-eyed look that could have been anything from amusement to pure terror. She still had the knife held straight out in front of her.

Stacia motioned for her to come on down. The woman cocked her head like she didn't understand. "Come on!" Stacia said. "We don't have much..." There was another burst of gunfire. Stacia ducked, even though it had apparently been directed at some woman in the corner who was crying mournfully that someone had gotten blood in her drink. Her protests ceased rather abruptly. "If you don't come down now, I'll have to leave you behind." It occurred to Stacia for the first time that maybe that was exactly what the woman wanted. After all, what did Stacia really have to offer her? She felt a strange desire to keep this peculiar woman safe, but could Stacia really give her any safety once she left Hobbes in search of Stanton? How many more vicious creatures were out there that would see her as a quick snack?

Before Stacia could voice any of these possibilities, the Skin hurried down the stairs. "I'm coming. But, um, where are we going?"

"We'll figure that out later. Right now, anywhere but here."

Stacia turned for the door just in time to see Mur charging at her. It wasn't enough time to dodge, though. Mur barreled Stacia over onto the floor, where they rolled for several seconds before Mur ended up on top of her. She thrust her sonic blade down, aiming for Stacia's eyes. Stacia caught her wrist and tried to hold Mur back, but the pit-fighter had obviously been keeping up with her training. Slowly, Stacia gave up valuable inches to Mur's strength, and the blade got closer, closer...

Then a completely different blade popped out of Mur's eye. Stacia didn't understand what was happening at first. Did Mur have some kind of weird additional implant that allowed her to sprout another weapon from her head? But as Mur worked her mouth, trying to speak, blood flowed down her face along with pieces of her eye. Definitely not intentional. Stacia pulled out from under her as she dropped forward, revealing the Skin woman over her, the sonic blade Stacia had given her now jammed into the back of Derre Mur's head.

The woman's mouth hung open in horror at what she had done, and Stacia had no doubt that she would have continued standing there uncomprehendingly until someone else finally came along and knifed her in the back. Stacia stood up and shook her out of her stupor.

"Come on!" As Stacia pulled the knife out of Mur's head, the woman finally blinked and seemed to realize she was in even more danger now than before. Previously, she had just been yet another Skin caught in the fight. Now, she had actively taken the life of one of her masters. If there had been any way for the woman to stay behind, it was completely gone now.

Faust had somehow gotten lost in the fight, leaving the door just open enough for the two of them to run through with a minimum of kicking and punching on the way. Outside in the mostly deserted street, a single Elite stood in Stacia's way with a plasma pistol pointed at her. The Elite might not have been wearing his armor anymore, but he would still have the neural implants and all the enhanced reflexes and perceptions that came with it. Now that Stacie was closer, she could clearly see the scars on the exposed skin where it has been cut off some other helpless fellow and reattached onto him. Not that she had had reason to doubt her companion's story before now, but this proved the horrible fate of many that were born naturally on Leviathan.

The Elite nodded at her, then indicated his pistol, then indicated her 808 and shook his head. Stacia understood what he meant. A duel. It would be crazy and stupid to actually agree to this. Without the armor, the Elite would probably be faster on the draw. Yet she also knew that, if she tried to use her 808 at the moment, he'd be able to get her first. Silently, Stacia nodded to the man in agreement, lowered her 808, and hit a switch on it. She turned to the Skin.

"I need you to hold my rifle while I take care of this." She thrust the weapon into the startled woman's hands. "Just hold it in his general direction and squeeze the trigger if he tries to do anything outside the rules."

"I don't even know the rules."

"I don't think there are any." Keeping her back to the Elite and moving slowly, Stacia stepped aside from the Skin and then slowly pulled out a pistol and held it at her side.

"If you don't think there are any rules, then why are you following them?" the woman asked.

"I'm not." The switch that she had flipped on the 808 clicked. A burst of fire came out of the rifle, scaring the Skin enough that she dropped the weapon. Stacia spun around to see that, while most of the bullets had missed the Elite, one had hit him in the leg and the other in the chest. Stacia fired off two more shots from the pistol, both of them hitting him in the head and melting his face. The Elite never even raised his gun.

Stacia picked up the 808. "Next time, hold on to it."

"Uh, okay."

Stacia grabbed the Elite's body and slung it over her shoulder. The Skin would need clothes, but they didn't have time to strip the corpse just now. They instead had to get as far away from Hobbes as possible.

As the ran over the tiny metal wall, the Skin hesitating ever so slightly as though she thought whatever might be beyond was worse than her fate might be if she stayed, Stacia looked back at the center building. Lexton stood near the door with Faust. Neither of them gave chase and neither of them had weapons, but Lexton shaped her finger into a gun and pantomimed pulling the trigger.

The parting message was obvious.

8
HOME ON THE STRANGE

The Skin was not used to running, especially not in the wide open uneven ground. She tired quickly, so Stacia had her climb up on her back for a time as Stacia continued to put some distance between them and Hobbes. After about two hours of this, and with the sun beginning its descent to the horizon, Stacia realized she wouldn't be able to keep this up anymore without food and rest. So they stopped to make camp, and Stacia was finally able to take stock of the situation.

Knowing full well now what kind of threats lurked among the barnacle/tree-things, Stacia had gone straight out over the open plain until the forest of barnacles could no longer be seen. The only thing there was to see for kilometers in every direction was the alien grass and the occasional strange trail of dead earth winding among it. She would be able to see or hear any danger approaching. They also didn't have any shelter. Stacia had no idea how cold this area of Leviathan got at night. The elements could only do so much to harm her, but her unexpected companion was another issue.

The woman got down from her perch on Stacia's shoulders, hugging her arms tight to her breasts either to keep herself warm or in some attempt at modesty. Given what she had been doing when Stacia found her, Stacia's guess was the former. She stripped the clothes off the dead Elite and handed them to the woman, then tossed the body well off to the side away from their meager camp. She had no idea what kind of scavengers a dead body might attract, but she didn't have the means to bury it or otherwise dispose of it at the moment.

The woman wordlessly dressed, although the simple shirt, pants, and boots combo managed to look even more ridiculous on her slight and malnourished frame than she had when she was butt naked. There was also the fact that the shirt and pants had bullet holes and blood on them, but the woman didn't seem to mind. Stacia figured she'd probably seen worse.

When the woman was finished, she stood stock still, still trembling slightly, waiting for Stacia to tell her to do something.

"Don't you want to sit down?" Stacia asked.

"Is that what you would like me to do?"

"It doesn't matter what I would like you to do. What do *you* want to do?"

She looked shocked by this question. "Is this a test?"

Stacia raised an eyebrow at her but didn't respond. Instead, she sat down herself, and after several seconds of indecision, the woman followed suit.

"Okay, before we do anything else," Stacia said, "we're going to have to figure out your name."

The woman shook her head. "Skins don't have names."

"Yeah, you said that. But I can't just keep calling you Skin, can I?"

"Why not?"

"Unless that's what you want me to call you?"

The woman cocked her head and thought about it. "Are you going to kill me?" She said it very calmly, as though a *yes* answer wouldn't be that terrible.

"Of course not."

"Why not?"

"Because I don't have a reason to."

"You killed lots of people at the Head House."

"That's because they got in my way."

"If I get in your way, are you going to kill me?"

Stacia took a long time to respond. "I don't want to do that. That's why I brought you with me. After talking to you, I couldn't just leave you there. But I have something I need to do. Something very important to me. Something I intend to do no matter what. My advice to you is, don't get in my way, and neither of us will have to find out the answer to that question."

That seemed to satisfy her. "So you're not going to eat me?"

"What? No." Stacia didn't want to ask why that question would even occur to her.

"And you're not going to take my skin?"

"No."

"Then yes."

"Yes what?"

"Yes, I want to be called Skin. If you promise me I get to keep it, that's what I want to be."

Stacia shrugged. "Okay then. I promise."

The woman gave Stacia the first genuine smile she had seen since crashing on this gods-forsaken planet. She waved frantically in greeting, even though she was less than a meter away. "Hi! I'm Skin!"

Stacia smiled back. "Nice to meet you, Skin. I'm Stacia X-79."

Skin didn't seem to think there was anything strange about a woman having nothing but numbers and letters as a last name. Come to think of it, given the way people like her were treated on this world, Stacia wouldn't be surprised if she'd never learned to even write numbers or letters.

"Okay then, Skin, now that we've got some time to talk, why don't you tell me what I need to know?"

She cocked her head again. "I don't know what you need to know."

"That's because I haven't asked you yet. When Faust brought me to Hobbes, he and the rest of his people looked nervous about getting too far away from the barnacles. Given that I've already seen what lives among the barnacles, maybe you could tell me what could possibly be so much worse that people would prefer keeping close to the dominatrixes."

Skin fidgeted and looked away. "Wet Lisa."

"Who's Wet Lisa?"

"I don't know."

"Tell me what you do know."

"It's not a who. It's a what. And there's a bunch of them, I think. I've never been allowed to leave Hobbes, so I haven't seen one. But I know they're the reason there's no grass around Hobbes."

"Why? What do they do to the grass?"

"I don't know. Most of the Shellheads I worked with wouldn't talk about them. Like it was bad luck."

"Okay. What else do you know about this Wet Lisa?"

"I know that's what ate the Lord Commander's face." She thought about it for a second. "And they only come out during the day. It's safe at night."

Stacia looked in the direction of the setting sun again. So they would be safe from whatever these things were. She couldn't get complacent, though. That also meant any searchers from Hobbes would probably be out and about in the dark.

"Oh, and they're named after the Lord Commander's mother," Skin said.

"Hmm. I'm not sure I want to know why Lexton called her mother Wet Lisa. But what about that wall? It seems to have worked, but I don't have the slightest clue how."

"I don't know," Skin said with a shrug. "That's not usually what the Shellheads talk about when they take me to bed. Usually, they just complained that it was unfair that they were on this planet."

Stacia quizzed Skin on as much as she could regarding the planet, ranging from the length of the days to what local life might be edible to humans. On some things, Skin was helpful, like where to find the little bushy structures that made up the fiber for their clothing, while on other things, like anything about extended life outside of Hobbes, she was unclear on. If it hadn't been involved with something the Skins needed to do to serve the Shellheads, then it had never been taught to them. Finally, Stacia couldn't keep dancing around the subject and had to ask.

"Skin, how did this society even happen?"

"I don't understand what you mean."

"I mean, the Skins serving the Shellheads."

"That's just always the way it's been."

Stacia thought back to what little she already knew. Alena Lexton had been the first person sentenced to the radical idea of a prison planet exclusively for former Galactic Marines, and since she was still in charge, it stood to reason that she'd had a large part in making Leviathan (or at least Hobbes, she reminded herself, as Leviathan was a very big planet and Lexton was just one small woman) what it was. She didn't remember what Lexton had been sentenced for, but it had to be something horrible to introduce the idea of an entire planet set aside for people like her.

So it made some sense that Lexton would create a society where people like her ruled and others without her Galactic Marine enhancements were slaves. Sometimes a lot worse than slaves, from some of the things Skin had said. In addition to the natural born of the planet being harvested for their hides, Skin had said one or two things so far that led Stacia to believe that there might even be cannibalism. An entire group of human beings used as slave labor and sex toys at best, cattle at worst.

Stacia tried a different question. "Who were your parents?"

"Parents," Skin said thoughtfully. "I don't know if I had any."

"You must have. There doesn't appear to be the technology on this planet to do anything other than natural birth."

"Oh! You want to know who birthed me. That's different, but I don't know that either."

"Why don't you know? And why do you think that's different?"

"I don't know because I don't know. Parents aren't common. I was raised in a communal house like all the other kids. And it's different because parents aren't allowed."

"Explain that."

Skin looked at her like Stacia was the naïve one that needed to learn the basic facts of the universe. "When anyone gets pregnant, they're not allowed to see the baby. It gets taken away right away."

"This may be a planet full of the worst offenders the galaxy has to offer, but I refuse to believe that every single one of them allow that. There's got to be a lot of them with parental instincts."

"There are plenty that wish they could keep their babies. But they can't. The Skins know better than to try anything, but every so often, a Shellhead thinks they can take their babies and run away before anyone can stop them."

"And what happens then?"

Skin shrugged. "No one ever sees them in Hobbes again."

"What about you? Have you ever had a baby?"

Stacia regretted the question the instant a haunted look came over Skin's face. "I was pregnant once."

That wasn't exactly an answer. Stacia waited to see if Skin would elaborate, but she just sat in silence. Stacia decided to let it go.

"So you really have no idea who your mother and father are?"

"No. Well, maybe. There was one time. Right after they made me start working on the stages in the common house. A Shellhead told me to come with him upstairs, and I figured he was going to do the usual things to me. But he didn't. He had me sit on the bed and just looked at me for several minutes, then said he was done and left. He was killed by a dominatrix soon after. Normally, that kind of thing doesn't bother me. It happens, and I've spent lots of times with lots of Shellheads. But him, I don't know, I felt sad afterward." Skin stared off into the distant twilight for a few seconds, then looked at Stacia. "So is that something that happens on other worlds? People know their parents?"

"Maybe not everyone," Stacia said. "There are a lot of worlds, a lot of sentient creatures, a lot of ways of life. But for me, I know my mothers well."

Skin tilted her head. "Mothers? No father?"

"Yes and no. I don't know which of my mothers is my

biological mother. They insist it doesn't matter, that they both love me like I was in their womb. They were in love and wanted a child, so they enlisted a friend to be the biological father. He lived with us and helped them raise me until I was five."

"Did he leave?"

"No. He died." Stacia stopped, unsure if she wanted to continue. She was a Galactic Marine. Marines weren't supposed to dwell on the past or attachments. Except she wasn't really a marine anymore, was she? It might feel good to say these things to someone, especially someone she didn't have to worry about getting in her way. "All three of my parents had military training. But Papa didn't have the same level of combat experience. So when some rebels attacked my homeworld, and the various branches of the service fought back, he got caught in a building he shouldn't have been in when it was shelled. Completely vaporized."

"I'm... I'm sorry?" Skin asked, as though she wasn't sure if this was the correct response for this sort of thing. "Did... did your mothers both live?"

"They lived, and they went back to duty. They felt like they had to. Especially after..." No, Stacia thought. She couldn't go that far. That much she had to keep to herself.

"After what?" Skin asked. Apparently, she didn't know what a *hint* was.

Stacia continued, choosing every word carefully. "The ionic mortar shell that hit the building belonged to the Galactic Marines. Now, the rebels were using a lot of tech they had stolen from various armed services, so no one could be certain exactly where it came from. But there was a lot of evidence someone on our own side fired it with no regard for what it would do to civilians. My mothers came out of their semi-retirement because they wanted to root out anyone that might have been involved. And they had that power. Because they were both generals."

Skin looked a little confused at the term "generals," but she at least seemed to understand they were people with power.

"And not just any generals, either. Some of the most decorated generals of all time. They became famous even before then for some of their actions when they were just raw Galactic Marine recruits. Back then, there were a few units designated by just letters and numbers. Mama Gertrude was part of Unit X-7. Mama Linny was in Unit X-9."

Skin perked up. "That's where your name comes from!"

Stacia nodded. "When they got married, they both kept their last names, Gertrude Abrams and Linsel Mockmone. But when I came along, they couldn't decide which surname to give me, and they wanted to do something different anyway, so my official last name became a combination of their unit designations. With that kind of history, it was a foregone conclusion that I would follow in the footsteps of my parents and join the Galactic Marines."

"But... you're not one anymore? At least, according to you?"

"No, I'm not. I betrayed the Galactic Marine Corps. I'm no longer deserving of that title."

"Why? What did you do?"

"I shot my superior officer."

"On purpose?"

"Yes. Repeatedly."

"I still don't understand. I haven't even known you for a day, but that already seems like something you wouldn't do. Especially given how dedicated you are to the Galactic Marines."

Stacia thought for a long moment, took a deep breath, and then looked Skin in the eyes. "General Borealis was the one responsible for the shelling of my home. My father died because of her actions, and she has kept that fact hidden from the public for years. I found out, but I couldn't prove it."

"So you killed her?"

"I shot her, but she lived. I was already taken into custody by the time I found out she was going to make it, so I decided to do the next best thing. She took someone special from me, so I'm going to take someone important from her."

"Is that where we're going? Is that what that leather says that you keep looking at?"

"Yes. The location of Stanton Borealis. Her last living child.

He crashed here but couldn't get off, because—"

"No one gets off of Leviathan," Skin finished for her. Her voice had a reverent tone, like this was sacred scripture she had been forced to repeat for her entire life.

"No one leaves," Stacia agreed.

"Does he deserve it? This Stanton person?"

Stacia didn't answer. Skin didn't seem to like that.

"So you're going to kill someone that doesn't deserve it."

"His mother deserves it."

"But he doesn't." There was something interesting about the way she said it, like she wanted to challenge Stacia on this but was afraid and didn't know what Stacia would do in retaliation.

"You're entitled to your opinion," Stacia said, hoping Skin would take that to mean both that she should stop talking like that, yet she wouldn't be punished if she didn't. Whether or not Skin took the hint, she remained quiet until the night was fully upon them and she fell asleep in the grass. Stacia contemplated starting a fire, but decided against it. The fire would be an obvious beacon for anyone looking for them, and Stacia herself didn't need it. Between her implants and her armor, she could survive comfortably in temperatures up to forty below zero, and uncomfortably in even colder. Skin would need warmth, but Stacia could provide that for her just by sleeping nearby. She set her implants to wake her when either the sky started to lighten or they sensed unexpected movement nearby, then she too went to sleep.

Less than an hour later, it wasn't the sun that woke her up. Stacia's implants set off alarms in her brain as she sensed something touching her. She grabbed the sonic blade she'd been sleeping with and immediately put it the neck of the intruder, only to find that the intruder was Skin herself. The woman had huddled up close to Stacia, but that wasn't what had set off Stacia's warnings. Instead, the woman had her lips just centimeters away from Stacia's, and her hand was at Stacia's legs, working the hatch the covered her crotch. Both of them froze, Stacia fighting her every instinct to slice the throat of someone who'd come after her in her sleep, and Skin trembling slightly, her lip quivering.

"Please do it quickly," Skin said.

"I won't hurt you if you tell me what the hell you're doing."

"I... I thought... maybe you wanted me to do this. You claimed me as yours by taking me. I figured this was why." Her hand tried to work its way into the opening below in Stacia's armor. Stacia jerked her hips away and pressed the knife tighter to Skins throat. All she needed to do was operate the sonic function, and the knife would practically push itself through the woman's jugular.

"I did not give you permission," Stacia said.

Skin closed her eyes. A single tear ran down her cheek. Clearly, she expected to die any moment now.

Stacia pulled the blade away and stabbed it into the dirt nearby, close enough that she could still grab it if she needed but far enough away her message would be clear. Skin paused for a second before backing away.

"I'm not one hundred percent sure why I took you with me," Stacia said. "I think I felt sorry for you, although I don't know I'll be able to give you anything better than what you had. I thought I made it clear in that bedroom, though, that I have no interest in using you for sex. Even if you didn't feel obligated. Because you're not obligated to do anything anymore, not as long as the two of us are watching out for each other."

"So... I don't have to have sex with you? At all."

"No."

"Is there something wrong with me?"

"No, absolutely not."

Skin nodded in understanding. "It's because I'm a woman. You're one of those people that's only attracted to men."

"No, I'm not attracted to men either."

"But I'm confused. Who or what are you attracted to, then?"

"Nobody. Not in that way. I have no interest in sleeping with anyone for any reason other than safety and warmth in numbers."

"Did something happen to you? Is it because of watching your father die? Did that break something inside you?"

"There's nothing wrong with me. The fact that I have no

interest in sex does not make me broken, any more than you wanting it would make you broken. Neither of us is broken. We are whole in and of ourselves."

"So, you really don't want me to do anything to you?"

"No."

"Even if I wanted to?"

"Doesn't matter."

"Huh." Skin lay back down and stared up at the starry sky. "That's so strange. Is that the way things are on other planets?"

"Most of them."

"You have a choice. And I have a choice." She was silent for several seconds before saying "huh," again, and turning over to go back to sleep. Stacia watched her drift off to sleep, then moved close enough again for Skin to share her warmth before falling asleep herself.

This time, Stacia was uninterrupted until morning.

9
WET LISA

Stacia was awake before Skin, which gave her some time by herself to examine the piece of leather Lexton had given her in greater detail. Stacia supposed it could be fake, if Lexton had planned in advance to double cross her. However, she wasn't sure what Lexton thought she could gain by that. She wanted Stanton eliminated, as long as it couldn't be directly tied to Lexton herself, so it would actually be to Lexton's advantage if Stacia continued on her mission. The rough map on the leather, though, gave directions to some place called Roo-Soh, and it was clear that Lexton was familiar with it. So Lexton knew exactly where Stacia was going. No wonder they hadn't been followed in the night. Lexton would probably go directly to Roo-Soh and set a trap for Stacia, not to be sprung until after Stacia had completed her objective.

Stacia thought about this and tried to come up with a plan as the sun rose over the edge of the horizon. Skin yawned and smacked her lips.

"I don't suppose we know how we're going to eat?" Skin asked.

Stacia absently reached into her pack and pulled out some of the rations she had arrived with. There weren't enough for one person to eat for more than five days, but Stacia could force herself to go without eating for a while if she had to. Skin wouldn't have the same training and enhancements. Besides, the young woman looked like she desperately needed some meat on her bones.

Skin immediately shoved the food in her mouth, thought for a second, and then spoke around a mouth full of crumbs. "Thunk yuh."

Stacia nodded, trying not to let Skin see her smile.

"Roo-Soh isn't actually that far away," Stacia said as she put the leather back in her pack. "We should be able to make it by this time tomorrow, I think."

"And then you kill this Stanton person?" Skin asked quietly. Stacia only nodded.

"What then?" Skin asked.

"We'll come to that when we get there," Stacia said. "We don't want to count our chickens before they're hatched."

"What's a chicken?"

"Something that gets hatched."

"Oh. Uh, okay."

Stacia stood up and made sure she had everything she needed packed. "Let's get going."

"Do you need me to carry one of those? They look heavy," Skin said, pointing at Stacia's two 808s.

"They are, but not too heavy for me."

"Can I carry one anyway?"

Stacia smiled. "I suppose. Just don't shoot me by accident."

"Uh, I'll try not to. If I do, please don't kill me."

"For the last time, Skin, I'm not going to..." Stacia trailed off as she looked around at the matted-down grass that had been their camp. "Uh, Skin?"

"What?"

"Did you move the body of that Elite that we brought with us?"

"No. Why would I do that?"

"I don't know. But it's gone."

Stacia stared at the spot where she was sure she had dumped

the body. She hadn't wanted it stinking up their camp, so she had given it some distance, but not so much distance that she would have lost its location in the tall grass. There was something different, though, about the spot where Stacia had placed it. There was a path, leading both to and away from the spot, where the grass was completely gone. All that was left there was the bare dirt.

"Skin, don't move," Stacia said. "I don't think we're alone."

"Is it a Wet Lisa?" Skin asked. Stacia could only shrug. She still didn't have the slightest clue what that meant. Given the size of the planet's fauna that she had met so far, though, she was surprised that, whatever had taken the body, it hadn't tripped all her mental alarms already. There shouldn't have been anything that could get this close without her noticing.

Stacia's gaze followed the paths going from where the body had been. One seemed to clearly be the creature's approach, given that the grass-less trail came in from deeper on the plain. Going the other direction, Stacia saw the missing grass go around their camp in a wide circle. The grass was too high for her to see the ground, but she could clearly see the pattern it had been making. It was circling them, spiraling inward. Finally, she found the place where the path abruptly ended, with no sign of... wait.

As she watched, several stalks of the grass noiselessly toppled over and vanished from view. Then a few more.

The Wet Lisa, whatever the hell it was, was right there, and it was trying to create a circle around them. Looking at its pattern, the circle of missing vegetation was about to be complete. Stacia had a feeling they didn't want to be inside that circle when it was.

"Skin, run!"

"Run where?" Skin, who hadn't quite made the connection yet that something bad was about to happen, stood in place, looking frantically around her for a danger she couldn't see. As the Wet Lisa got closer to completing the circle, Stacia noticed something else: the island of grass at the center of the circle was getting smaller. Whatever was on the outside of the circle was beginning to creep in.

Stacia tried to use her tactical implants to get some idea what she was dealing with, but they were coming up with curiously little data. The implants kept trying to say that they must be surrounded by insects, some kind of locust-like creature, but there was absolutely no sound. The thing or things didn't give off any heat or any smell. The only thing her implants could discern was that the air around them had grown slightly moister.

Resigning herself that the tactical implants would be of little help at the moment, Stacia ran up to Skin, grabbed her by the waist, and slung the woman over her shoulder. The noise of Skin's "oof!" was drowned out by the sudden rustling of all the grass around them, the sound of a heavy wind even though the air was completely still. Quicker than she'd expected, the last of the grass around the perimeter fell, connecting the circle. The vegetation dropped and disappeared quicker, closing in on them. Whatever these things were, Stacia's sudden movement had alerted them that they'd lost the element of surprise and now was the time to take their prey.

Stacia got the best running start she could, then jumped over the ever-widening dead space around them. She looked down for just a second, and finally her implants, now with some sensory data they could analyze, gave her an idea of what she was dealing with.

Stacia was a professional. She had dealt with more weird alien creatures, diabolical plots, and just plain strange occurrences than she could possibly count. But this one was so off her radar that she almost misjudged her landing and fell on the other side of her jump.

Wet Lisa was a puddle.

This? This is what everyone's so afraid of? Stacia thought. But even as that crossed her mind, the neural implants were doing their job, analyzing everything they had seen, everything she could sense, everything she had been told. The scenario that suddenly formed in her head was terrifying.

Wet Lisa (or was it the Wet Lisa? Wet Lisas? She still couldn't be sure if she was dealing with a single creature, one of many, or an entire colony) was a peculiar bright green color, completely flat, no visible appendages or sensory organs at all. But there was no doubt that it was alive in some fashion, because it was moving of its own will. Where it touched the grass, the grass immediately dissolved into it. It was like living acid, taking any shape it needed to surround its prey, and it grew with everything it ate.

And it had suddenly switched directions, no longer going for the center of the circle but the two juicy humans that had just jumped over it. Considering it was nothing more than a shimmering green puddle, the damned thing could move *fast*.

"Skin, can this thing be killed?" Stacia asked.

"I... oof, that hurts!" Skin said as Stacia bounded over a large stone in the ground and jostled the passenger draped over her shoulder. "I don't know! No one ever said anything about that!"

Stacia risked turning around for just a split second to get an idea of the creature's speed. It was almost as fast as her, but not quite. Stacia could probably outrun it if she had enough time and energy, but she had no idea what kind of stamina a puddle of goo might have.

She did notice that it flowed around the rock she'd jumped over rather than sliding over it. Her neural implants immediately took that information and began calculating, processing...

"Hey, I think I can shoot it," Skin said. Stacia had almost forgotten until now that Skin still held one of the 808s.

"Wait, I don't think—" Before she could finish, Skin squeezed the trigger, and a flurry of bullets fanned out behind Stacia. Skin screeched, still not used to the kickback.

"Uh oh," Skin said. Stacia didn't need to ask her what had happened. She felt the weight on her shoulder lessen as Skin dropped the weapon. "I'm sorry! I'm sorry! I'm..."

Stacia stopped dead and turned around to face the Wet Lisa. She watched the 808 fall and flatten the grass, which the creature immediately swarmed. The grass appeared to melt into the Wet Lisa. The 808 didn't do anything.

"Stacia, what are you doing?" Skin screamed. "We need to—"

"Stay. Completely. Still," Stacia said. With a final lunge, the Wet Lisa flowed forward and around Stacia's metal boots.

Nothing happened.

The Wet Lisa continued flowing toward them until they were completely surrounded by a twenty-foot wide pool of the green slime. Everywhere it touched the grass, the vegetation disappeared into the puddle of primordial sludge. And yet, as Stacia stood in the middle of it, the Wet Lisa did nothing to hurt her.

"Wait, what's happening?" Skin asked.

With her free arm, Stacia reached up to her head and yanked out a single strand of her hair. Holding it over the slime, she watched the Wet Lisa bubble and bulge slightly underneath the hair, as though it could sense a piece of juicy human. Stacia let go, and the hair dissolved instantly in the creature.

"Organic material," Stacia said. "It can only absorb organic material."

"What does that mean?" Skin asked.

"It means that if I set you down in this slop, you would melt into it. If I put my face in it, that would get eaten, too. But the inorganic polymer/metal alloy of my armor? It can't do anything about that. Right now, to this thing, I'm a meal in a can, and it doesn't have a can opener."

The green slop made some kind of pulsating move at her toes, like it was trying to find a way to grip and slip up the boot until it could find a crack in which to slide and take the meat within. But apparently, the Wet Lisa hadn't evolved for that.

"That explains that silly wall around Hobbes," Stacia said. "As long as it's metal, it doesn't matter how high it is. The Wet Lisa doesn't have any way to get over it."

"So what does this mean?"

Careful not to jostle Skin too much, Stacia plodded through the Wet Lisa to the dropped 808 and then bent to pick it up. The footprints she left behind in the goop closed up quickly, and the slime where she stepped fled from her boot. Holding the 808 in her free hand, Stacia inspected it to see if the Wet Lisa had left any damage or remnants of itself. There were a couple of small bits in the handle, where the faux-leather grip wasn't completely made from synthetic materials. But otherwise, the weapon looked completely fine. Just to be sure, she had Skin yank another hair from Stacia's head and place it where the gun had been bathed in the creature. The hair didn't react.

"It means that you're safe," Stacia said to Skin. "As long as you don't touch the ground."

Stacia took a few more steps. The Wet Lisa both gave way to her and followed, keeping itself around her at all times just in case she might drop something tasty in it.

"Are you going to be able to carry me all day?" Skin asked.

"It doesn't look like I have any choice. I'm certainly not going to drop you in it, so don't worry about that."

"Do you think it will go away when it gets dark out?"

Stacia thought that was a possibility. Although this was an alien planet with alien biology, the Wet Lisa's green color implied to Stacia that it might by photosynthetic, using the energy from the sun to sustain some of its functions. That would explain why no one ever seemed to be worried about these things at night.

"Probably," Stacia said. "But we're going to move carefully. Do you think you can get into a more comfortable position on me? Maybe ride on my shoulders?"

The next few minutes probably would have looked comical, had anyone been around to witness it and had a dark sense of humor. Stacia did her best to rearrange her gear on her back even as Skin crawled around on her, trying to get into a more sustainable riding position without her actually being able to touch the ground. There were a couple close calls, one where Skin slipped and caught Stacia's armor just before her toe dipped into the slime, and the other where Stacia herself almost lost her balance. Once they were finished, though, they'd managed to create something that was almost a saddle using the two 808s on Stacia's back and her pack.

"You probably look like you're riding a horse," Stacia said.

"What's a horse?" Skin asked.

"It's something that goes good with steak sauce, if you're

desperate."

"Oh. Uh, I still don't know what any of that means."

Stacia finally started trudging off across the plain, the Wet Lisa surrounding her, on her way to Roo-Soh. The creature was almost like a pet, if the only reason the pet stuck around was to eat its owner's face at the earliest opportunity.

"This is going to get old quickly," Stacia said.

10

ROO-SOH

They had to make much slower time than Stacia had hoped, given that she still had a fear of slipping in the Wet Lisa and both of them being dead before they had realized they'd fallen. Even with her armor-augmented body, Stacia felt the drain of carrying another person all the way across the plains after several hours. She actually had to stop and take a brief nap at one point, a prospect that had scared the hell out of Skin. Stacia, however, didn't actually need to lie down to sleep. There was a feature in the armor that allowed the marine inside to sleep standing up, designed for those times when the Galactic Marines had to go into swampy environments and laying down might result in drowning. When Stacia woke, she found Skin also out cold, slumped forward on Stacia in the perfect position to drool all over Stacia's head. Stacia patiently wiped the drool away, then woke Skin up and proceeded on their way.

Late in the day, the Wet Lisa started to lose ground. Stacia found that, even at her less than hurried pace, it still could not keep up a distance of ten feet around her in all directions. Part of that was probably from the sun, which was getting lower again, but also part of it was probably because of the change in terrain. The plains were giving way more and more to rocky outcroppings jutting from the earth, and with that, the vegetation became less dense. With less light and not as much to feed on, Stacia didn't think the Wet Lisa would continue its dogged pursuit for much longer. Finally, it stopped altogether at a place where broken stones covered the ground almost completely. Stacia stopped, waiting to see what it would do. The Wet Lisa moved back and forth over the ground like it was pacing at a fence, then turned around (or rather just reversed direction, since it didn't have a back or front to turn) and went back onto the plains. Skin insisted on staying on Stacia's shoulders for a while longer, just in case this was some kind of trick and the Wet Lisa would be back, but finally Stacia insisted she had to get off. Sooner than Stacia had wanted to today, they made camp in the shadow of a cliff that looked like it had been shoved up out of the planet by some relatively recent cataclysmic earthquake.

"I was told there was a lot of seismic activity on Leviathan," Stacia said, "but I haven't witnessed any yet. Do earthquakes happen often?"

Skin cocked her head in an expression that Stacia was coming to know very well, the look of Stacia revealing that the worlds Skin had never seen were more foreign and bizarre than she could imagine. "Of course. You mean they don't happen all the time elsewhere?"

This led to a conversation until well after dark regarding the various worlds Stacia had visited and all the strange and amazing creatures she had seen (and very often killed soon afterward). Stacia fell asleep first, which surprised her when she woke in the morning. She hadn't realized she'd already become so accustomed to Skin's presence that she felt comfortable doing that. She was even more surprised to find Skin curled up not next to her, but next to a completely disassembled 808, complete with all its parts lined up in an orderly fashion. When Skin woke up, she was afraid Stacia would be angry with her. Instead, Stacia was intrigued and questioned why the young woman had done it. She said she hadn't wanted another incident like the one where she had dropped the weapon in the Wet Lisa, and she'd figured that if she had a better idea of what was inside it, she might know how to use it better. Stacia challenged her to put it back together, which Skin managed to do before she sun had completely risen. She wasn't as practiced and efficient with it as a trained Galactic Marine, but Stacia suspected that Skin's long time of servitude, being forced to take care of things behind the scenes where the Shellheads couldn't see, had given her the beginnings of all the knowledge she needed to work with complex machines. Stacia would need to remember that.

The earthquake ridge nearby, while apparently rather recent in a geological sense, was on the rough instructions Lexton had given her to reach Roo-Soh. According to them, Stacia and Skin were close to their destination. Stacia felt her first tremor on the planet while they were packing up and eating, although Skin said it wasn't even worth noticing. Once they were ready, the two of them followed the cliff for nearly a kilometer before Stacia finally got her first sight of the town.

"What is that?" Skin asked as they got their first view of the structures in the distance.

"I'm assuming it's the town of Roo-Soh."

"It doesn't look anything like Hobbes."

"Skin, I know you were probably raised to believe Hobbes was a bustling urban metropolis, but it's really just a pit. Wait until you see a real city."

"Is this a real city?"

"Not quite."

"Then I don't understand how I'll ever see one."

Stacia didn't answer that. Instead, she climbed up onto a nearby rock outcropping to get a better look at Roo-Soh. While Stacia could see now why someone had chosen to put Hobbes right at the boundary between the barnacles and the plains, this seemed like a much more sensible spot to attempt building a civilization. The people of Roo-Soh had taken a clue from certain ancient Earth cultures and carved their squat homes directly into the rocks of the cliff. Most of them could only be reached by a series of rough-hewn ladders and catwalks. There was still plenty of evidence that this was a town of former Galactic Marines in the form of repurposed drop pod pieces scattered all over.

"Why would they build like that?" Skin asked.

"It's the perfect defensible position. Nothing can get at them from behind them because of the cliff at their backs. And anyone approaching them from the front has the disadvantage of coming at them from lower ground. Any attacking party would probably get chewed up and spit out."

"If it's so perfect, why wasn't Hobbes made here?"

"I suspect that what they gain in defense, they lose in uncertainty. This area is obviously less geographically stable. Get a big enough earthquake, and the whole town could come tumbling down with the people still inside."

"I think I'd prefer Hobbes," Skin said.

"Don't be so quick to assume that," Stacia responded. "Especially considering... that."

Stacia pointed at some movement at the hovel closest to them. There was a woman working outside, a Skin. It looked like she was burying some kind of bowl in a shallow pit, which she looked like she would then set fire to. A makeshift kiln, probably. The Skin had dark skin from time in the sun, and while she didn't look like she'd lived an entirely easy life, she at least had the muscles of someone who had actual nutrition in her favor. A man came out of the hovel behind her, a Shellhead, and approached the woman. Stacia watched Skin wince at his approach, obviously expecting the woman to be beaten or berated at any second. Instead, the woman stood up from her work, kissed the man. The man stooped for a moment to help her with some of the burying. Then the woman waved good-bye to him as he made his way off down one of the catwalks.

The morning air was disturbed by the wail of a baby or small child from inside the hovel. The woman went in to investigate and disappeared from sight.

"It looks like things you were told about Skins serving the Shellheads aren't universally believed on Leviathan," Stacia said. Skin wasn't the only one staring at the scene with a new understanding. Stacia herself began to realize exactly what "ideas" Stanton Borealis probably professed if this was where he had chosen to live.

Or perhaps chosen wasn't the right word. Some distance away, Stacia could see the remains of a small ship. The state of it suggested that it hadn't landed so much as crashed, not that it could be taken off the planet even if it could be repaired. Instead, it looked like the people of Roo-Soh had been stripping it for parts.

"That right there," Stacia said, pointing at the ship's remains. "That was Borealis's ship."

"How do you know for sure?"

"Most of the conveyances that leave people on Leviathan are drop pods. Actual full-sized ships are rare."

"Still, couldn't it belong to someone else?"

"It's his. I know it."

Skin hesitated, then quietly said, "You don't have to do it."

"Skin, I came to Roo-Soh to accomplish something, and I intend to do it."

"But why? How do you know he deserves what you're going to do to him?"

"I know. More than you think."

"Is there something else you're not telling me?"

Stacia ignored the question. "Now we just need to figure out how we're going to approach the town."

"What do you mean?"

"I mean, I already said how hard it would be to sneak in. But there has to be a way."

"Why not just walk up and say hi?" With that, Skin started moving.

"Skin, no, wait, that's not..." Skin waved her arms. Before Stacia could pull her back, a Shellhead that had been descending one of the ladders saw her and called up to raise an alarm. A number of people appeared both along the cliff and from hidey-holes on the ground, all of them aiming weapons at the two of them. Stacia's tactical implants instantly took note of the fact that all of them were armed with nothing more than bows and arrows, makeshift crossbow, and other primitive and crude projectile throwers.

Interesting, Stacia thought. *Looks like Hobbes was the only place that benefited from Faust's little weapons deal*. She made a snap judgment and raised her hands in the air. "Don't shoot! We're friendly!"

Stacia thought she heard one of the approaching people chuckle at that. "Friendly" probably wasn't a word they used for many outsiders around here. The woman that came up to them first was a Skin, and judging from the way she ordered some of the others about, she must have had some authority.

"Yeah, we'll see. Name and rank, marine."

Stacia raised an eyebrow. With that kind of introduction, she would have guessed that this woman was an Elite, yet nothing showing anywhere on her exposed skin indicated that she'd taken it from someone else.

"Stacia X-79. And I don't have a rank. Not anymore."

"Sure you don't. Not the first time we've had someone from Hobbes try that one. Mind telling me... hey, stop that!" Skin, apparently noticing the same discrepancy Stacia had, was poking the woman in the neck and cheek.

"You're a Skin!" Skin said. "A real Skin! With a weapon and everything!" She tried to grab the woman's wrist to take a closer look at it, but the woman jerked it away.

"Sorry about that," Stacia said. "She has boundary issues. It's not her fault. I'm trying to teach her."

"Hmm," the woman said noncommittally. After several seconds of indecision, she lowered her weapon. Everyone else that had come with her followed suit.

"Did I say something that convinced you?" Stacia asked.

"No, but most Shellheads out of Hobbes don't come with a Skin that's not on a leash or something. Not that most Skins make it across the plains without getting melted."

"We came close," Skin muttered.

"X-79?" the woman asked. "Is that..."

"Yes, that's really my surname, and no, I'm not in the mood to rehash the story again."

"Hmm," the woman said again. "I'm Cobble Dossen. Current elected leader of Roo-Soh."

"Elections," Stacia said. "How droll."

"Yes, I'm guessing you've already been through Hobbes then. All the more reason you'll understand if we remain cautious. You must be fresh to Leviathan?"

"I was just discharged two days ago."

Cobble looked at the weapons strapped to Stacia's back and the blood that still covered Skin's clothes. "Looks like it's been an eventful two days."

"You have no idea."

"No, I'm pretty sure I do." Cobble turned and gestured for the other armed guards to head back to their posts. "Come on. Let's get you situated."

"Let me guess, I have to swear loyalty to you and Roo-Soh before I can do anything else."

Cobble actually laughed. "You really have been through Hobbes. No, you don't have to worry about that. But there's someone here that I'm pretty sure would like to meet you."

Stacia tensed, but tried not to let anyone else see. The tactical implants in her head started to work, and the conclusions they were drawing weren't happy. Especially now that they were starting to point out ways people could have gotten through Roo-Soh's meager defenses.

As nonchalantly as she could, Stacia slipped one of the plasma pistols into her hand, then did her best to make it look non-obtrusive. Nothing to see here, folks, move along. Definitely not expecting a double-cross at any moment.

Cobble led them over a number of ladders and catwalks in a switchback, zig-zag pattern until they were at the top-most building on the cliff. A little extra care had been taken into its design, leading Stacia to believe it was either Cobble's version of a mansion or some kind of government building. They went through the leather curtain that served for a door (not human, as far as Stacia could tell, but rather the stitched together pieces of a small, greenish animal) into a wide and tall room, lit by a hole near the top of one wall to let the sunlight through.

Stacia was completely and utterly unsurprised to find ten Shellheads in the room, each with 808s pointed directly at Stacia's head.

11
PAYBACK TIME

Skin immediately started freaking out and asking what was going on. Stacia, on the other hand, didn't even bother to give the marines a second look, even as they came up to her and removed every single one of her weapons all the way down to the sonic blade. Instead, she was taking in the features of the room, making sure she had ever detail.

There were a number of tables that had been shoved aside into one corner, leading Stacia to think that this place might be used as a communal food hall. Or maybe it was Roo-Soh's equivalent of the bar back in Hobbes. There were no naked people dancing in here, though, and no sign that these Shellheads were here to let loose some steam. Hanging from the walls on Stacia's left she saw a large number of what looked like maintenance tools, ranging from rough chisels to extra ladders and a number of sinewy ropes with hooks on the end. It made sense that the people here would need to regularly check for and repair any damage from the tremors, and that this might require some level of acrobatics and skill with ropes.

Stacia nodded almost imperceptibly to herself. No one seemed to notice, not even all the people looking like they wanted any excuse they could get to blow her head off.

"I'm sorry," Cobble said. One of the Shellheads had already

pulled her off to the side and had his 808 pointed at her.

"Let me guess," Stacia said. "Lexton's people got here shortly before we did?"

"Early last night," Cobble said.

"And maybe they're holding someone close to you? Someone to guarantee that you would cooperate and lead me into a trap."

"They have my husbands."

"That's okay. I understand. I promise, I won't kill you after I've finished killing all of them. I can't guarantee that you won't bleed out from your injuries, though."

Cobble looked confused. "Um, thank you?"

"Actually, given the mess she left behind in Hobbes, I'd take that seriously," someone said from just outside the door. Faust stepped in. In one hand, he had a plasma pistol. With the other, he pushed in Stanton Borealis.

Stacia had never actually seen the younger Borealis in person. The few pictures she had seen made him look handsome, if someone was into tall and lanky and angular. It was kind of difficult to tell that now, though, as his face was marred with blue and purple splotches where he'd met the business end of someone's fist. She presumed that someone was Faust, but there was no way to tell how many other enemies the man had made so far on this planet.

"Faust. Good to see you again," Stacia said. "I was looking forward to eventually ripping out your spleen. I didn't think I'd get to do it so soon."

"Miss X-79. The feeling's mutual."

"I'm assuming Lexton isn't far away?"

"You assume wrong," Faust said. "She'd be happier if she were around to witness you get what's coming for betraying her, but she's not stupid. On the off chance that you figure out a way out of this, she'd rather not be within firing range again."

"So she sends you instead. Guess that tells us what she thinks of you."

"It says that she knows I can do the job by myself."

"I'm sure it does." She nodded in Borealis's direction.

"Whatever happened to having someone kill him that couldn't be directly tied to Lexton?"

"She figured screw it. Originally, what she wanted was to take out Borealis and everyone else in Roo-Soh that advocated for Skins and Shellheads being equal, then slowly absorb the rest back into Hobbes. Mostly the Skins. She didn't want any Galactic Marines that might turn on her, while the Skins could just be, well, skinned immediately with no little trouble. The Skin of Hobbes would probably even welcome it. It would give them a reprieve for a while."

"Wait, what?" Cobble asked. "None of that was part of the..."

"Hey, you know what's kind of fun about this planet?" Faust asked Stacia. "They don't have the same knowledge of literature and pop culture that we do. So they don't see inevitable things like betrayal coming." Faust nodded to one of his Shellheads, who turned and casually shot Cobble in the stomach with a plasma pistol.

"Yeah, I saw that one coming," Stacia said.

Cobble dropped to her knees on the floor. The Shellhead must not have had the intensity on his plasma pistol turned up all the way, because that shot should have immediately melted every organ in that woman's gut. Instead, the outer skin was burned away, leaving most of the organs intact. The plasma had cauterized the wound, meaning that Cobble might actually live rather than bleed to death. Assuming she found a way to keep her intestines from spilling out. Cobble collapsed to the floor on her back as though she instinctively knew this.

"What happens now?" Skin asked timidly.

"Now we kill you, Borealis, and every person in Roo-Soh that we can't herd back to be used in Hobbes." Faust stopped and stared at Stacia's impassive face for a long time. "Does any of that bother you?"

"No, not really."

"You don't care that you're about to die? Or your friend?"

Stacia nodded toward Skin. "It's a shame about her, but otherwise, no. I don't know any of the people in this town. And I didn't think I was going to live too long on Leviathan anyway. All that really matters to me is that Stanton here goes down with me."

Faust smiled. "Rather pragmatic in your vengeance, aren't you."

"Why?" Stanton asked. His voice was hoarse and slurred thanks to his beating, but Stacia understood him just fine. "Why would you want to kill me? I haven't done anything."

"Everyone who's on this planet has done something to be here," Stacia said, then thought about it. "Okay, maybe not everyone. But you didn't just accidently show up in orbit over Leviathan and then happen to crash land."

"It was part of a protest! I was trying to bring attention to the fact that there were people on this planet who were innocent."

"But you didn't know that for certain."

"No, no one did, but we do now! Stacia, I've heard of you. I know who your mothers are. Is this really what they would want you to do? Kill someone who was trying to do good and ignore all the people in Hobbes being treated like cattle?"

"Don't presume to know what my mothers would and would not want me to do."

"Everyone, aim your weapons directly at Miss X-79's head," Faust said. Although a few of them looked confused by the order, every Shellhead in the room followed his directions.

"What's that about?" Stacia asked.

"You're going to die. No way around that. But how would you like to still get your revenge?"

"You're kidding, right?" Stacia asked.

"No, not at all." Faust took one of the plasma pistols back from a Shellhead and held it out to Stacia handle first. "Here. Go ahead. Take it."

Careful not to spook any of the Shellheads that might have itchy trigger fingers, Stacia took it.

"You can go ahead and kill him," Faust said. "Immediately after you pull the trigger, my people will blow your own head off. If you try to turn and aim at someone else, they will also blow your head off. Either way, your head's about to disappear. My advice to you would be to take advantage of this to get one last moment of enjoyment."

"I wouldn't say I'm going to enjoy any of this."

"Satisfaction, then."

For several seconds, every single person in the room was still and quiet, with the only exception being Cobble moaning on the floor. Slowly, Stacia raised the plasma pistol and put the barrel directly against Stanton's forehead. He closed his eyes.

"Stacia, no! Don't!"

"Skin, stay out of this."

"But he didn't do anything."

"I already told you. This isn't about anything he did. It's about what his mother did."

"He's innocent, though!"

"We're all about to die anyway. Why does it matter which one of us pulls the trigger on him?"

"Stacia, I've only known you for two days, but I know this can't be the real you. You believed in the Galactic Marines. You felt you had an honor and a duty to help people."

"Skin, stop. Just stop. I told you before, there's still more to this than I told you."

"Then tell me now! Make me understand!"

"God damn it, Skin. You really want to understand?"

"Yes."

"Really really?"

"Yes!"

"Fine then. Here's the truth."

Stacia ducked and swept her leg out in front of her, tripping Stanton and sending him sprawling on the floor. She'd counted on the Shellhead's complacency to lull them into a false sense of security while she and Skin argued, and thankfully, most of them obliged her. Two of the Shellheads, however, tracked her with their weapons as she dropped and fired. Stacia rolled out of the way, knocking down two more of the Shellheads at the same time. She felt a sharp, exploding pain as one of the bullets shredded her left ear, yet she suppressed her cry. Instead, she rolled to her feet, hit Faust in the face, and then fired five times at the Shellheads still on their feet. She got three in the head. One she hit in the chest, which sent him flying backward even though his armor absorbed most of the blast. With Faust on the floor, most of the Shellheads either dead or knocked out on the floor, and the rest rushing out through the door before Stacia could take them out, Stacia stood in the center of the carnage and nodded in appreciation at her own handiwork.

"Whuh?" Skin asked. She herself had ducked and run out of the way, hiding in a corner until Stacia's brief flurry of violence was finished. "Huh? I don't understand."

Stacia ignored her, instead walking calmly over to Stanton as he stared unbelievingly up at her from the floor. Stacia still had the pistol in one hand, but she kept it pointed well away from her target. Instead, she offered him the other hand to help him up.

"Stanton, your mother sent me. I'm here to get you off this shit-hole of a planet."

12
CLIFF RACING

"I don't know why I'm surprised," Stanton said as he took her hand and got back to his feet. "This is such a mother way of going about things."

"You sound like you don't approve," Stacia said.

"I wouldn't say that. It's just there had to be a more straightforward way."

"Could someone please explain to me what's happening?" Skin asked.

"Sorry, Skin. Wish I could, but I get the impression that whoever else came with Faust will be coming for us any minute now. I can explain once there's no one shooting at us."

"Is there ever a time when someone isn't shooting at you?" Stanton asked.

"Not really." She walked over to where Faust lay on the ground. He groaned but didn't move much. Stacia wondered if she had damaged something vital when she'd hit him.

"Should we tie him up?" Skin asked. "We could use those ropes to…"

Stacia shot Faust in the face. His head exploded in a wave of charred gore and green plasma.

"Oh," Skin said. "Um, never mind."

"Did you really have to do that?" Stanton asked.

"Yes," Stacia said. "I really did."

"There wasn't some less violent way to make sure he doesn't come after us?"

"It wasn't just about him coming after us. My neural implants calculated that there was little chance of getting you off world if he reported back to Lexton immediately that I've actually been here to save you this entire time. If he doesn't report exactly what he saw, the chances of pulling this mission off greatly improve. It was simple numbers."

"He was a man, not a number."

"Yeah? And she's a woman," Stacia said, pointing at Skin. "Yet you've seen what people like Faust have been doing to people like her. You go ahead and feel sorry for him all you want. Just remember where this..." She pulled out the piece of leather she'd used to find him and tossed it at his feet. "...actually came from."

"Is that...?"

"Yes."

"Jesus. I think I'm going to be sick."

"Get sick later. Escape now."

She quizzed him on what weapon he could operate best, but that was a lost cause. Stanton was a pacifist, an activist. She had been told as much when General Borealis had been preparing all this. Stanton had never fired a gun in his life. His preferred weapon was words. Words, unfortunately, would be pretty much useless in this situation. Stacia finally just forced a plasma pistol in his hand and hoped that he wouldn't burn off his own toes. To Skin, she gave one of the 808s. The other 808 she took over to the prone form of Cobble.

"I'm not going to live, am I?" Cobble asked. Stacia saw her internal organs jiggle as she spoke.

"I've actually seen people walk away with worse wounds."

"Really?" Cobble asked.

"No, not really at all. I was just trying to make you feel better. The plasma cauterization is keeping you from bleeding out, but your stomach honestly looks like the typical Galactic Marine without her armor. Unless you've got some spare armor lying around, you're pretty much gone."

"Please, you have to make sure that my husbands are safe."

"I'm not sure that I can make that promise. But if you do something for me, I can promise you this: when I get off this planet, I will make sure people stop ignoring what is happening to the Skins on Leviathan. Maybe something can change."

"Better than nothing, I guess. What do you need me to do?"

Using one of the ropes to bind up Cobble's wound and hopefully keep her insides from spilling out a little longer, Stacia propped her up where she had a clear, unobstructed view of the door. Then she gave Cobble the 808 and told her to shoot anyone or anything that came through the door.

"But what if it's one of my people?" Cobble asked.

"How many more of Lexton's Shellheads are there in the town?"

Cobble frowned. "Most of them were in here, but there were still some elsewhere keeping certain people from running."

"So they were guarding the important people? The ones who might come check if they thought something was wrong?"

"I see your point." Cobble looked at the extra controls on the side of the 808. "I don't know if I can operate this thing."

"Just ignore all the bells and whistles and pull the trigger when it's time."

"What about us?" Stanton said. "There's no way out. Lexton's people would be on the levels below waiting for us."

"That's why we're not going down," Stacia said. "We're going up."

She pointed high up at the wall. Both Skin and Stanton stared at the open window far above them at the top of a completely vertical surface.

"I can't climb up there," Stanton said. "I don't have the muscle strength to…"

Skin went over and grabbed the largest ladder she could find.

"Oh," Stanton said. "Right."

"Don't look too relieved," Stacia said as she went over to grab several of the ropes and hooks. "Your muscles are still going to get a workout. After the window, we're going to have to go straight up the cliff."

"I don't think I can make that climb," Stanton said.

"Me neither," Skin said.

"But I can," Stacia replied. "I already know that I can carry Skin for long distances. We're about to find out if I can do the same with both of you. Quick, climb up the ladder and wait for me at the window."

As they both went up, Stacia heard the roar of gunfire from behind. She didn't bother to look, instead concentrating on preparing the ropes. As long as the shots weren't heading her way, there was no use paying any attention to it. Cobble gave a guttural war scream as she held down the trigger, meant more to intimidate the enemy trying to get in the door. Stacia wasn't one for war cries herself, but she still approved.

Stacia did look down at the door once she was at the top of the ladder just to get an idea of how much time they had. Cobble fired blindly at any movement of the curtain, so no one had gotten in yet, but Stacia could hear voices from the other side conferring on what to do. She gave one last thumbs up to Cobble, who was too busy shooting to even notice, and then joined Stanton and Skin in the window ledge.

The window was roughly circular and cut into the stone at a slight downward angle to the outside so inclement weather was less likely to get in, but the wall was thick enough that all three of them could fit inside if they pushed together. Stacia shoved the ladder away, anything to give them just a little more time before they might be pursued.

"So what's the plan from here?" Stanton asked.

"Plan's a bit of a strong word. It's more like a general idea of how we might not die."

"Not dying sounds fun," Skin said. It was hard for Stacia to tell if she was being sarcastic. More likely, it was an honest and earnest assessment from the young woman.

"So what is it, then?" Stanton asked.

"Both of you are going to need to hang onto my back. I'll do my best to secure you with one of these ropes, but you can't assume it's going to hold, so don't lose your grip."

"And what are you going to do?" Stanton asked.

"I'm going to climb. I told you it wasn't much of a plan."

"And if someone sees us and shoots us?"

"We fall and die."

"This doesn't seem like a well thought-out rescue."

"It couldn't be. Our intelligence of everything happening on Leviathan's surface has been limited since the beginning. You're lucky you're getting a rescue attempt at all."

"Because no one leaves Leviathan," Skin said solemnly.

"Okay. Sorry," Stanton said. "I didn't mean to doubt you. If my mother trusts you, that should be good enough."

Skin started to speak. "I still don't understand why…"

"We'll fill in the plot holes later, Skin," Stacia said. "First, we've got to get through the action sequence."

Skin shook her head. "I don't understand what any of that means." She grabbed onto Stacia's back from the left side while Stanton did the same from the right. They held tightly to the shoulder pads of her armor as she lashed the rope around the three of them several times. Between the two of them and the weapons and pack she still had strapped to her back, movement through the window became infinitely more awkward.

Behind them, Cobble's gunfire abruptly stopped. Whether she had died or ran out of bullets, that was still Stacia's signal that it was time for them to go.

Keeping one plasma pistol and one hook and length of rope tucked where she could easily get them in the rope around her, Stacia slowly came out into the sunlight and surveyed the situation around her. On the various ledges and catwalks below, a fight had broken out between Lexton's people and the citizens of Roo-Soh. Lexton's Shellheads appeared to be broken up into two small groups, one consisting of the few that had run out the door after Stacia's attack, and other somewhat larger group much farther down the cliff. The ones up here had the high ground, and the lower ones looked like they had hostages, but in between, the combined Skins and Shellheads who called this place their home were putting up a hell of a fight despite their inferior weapons. Stacia felt a small pang that she couldn't be down there helping them. But helping people other than Stanton had never been part of this mission. The best she could do for everyone who didn't deserve to be here was simply to tell the rest of the galaxy that they existed at all.

Still, Stacia couldn't help but notice a single Shellhead near the top of the lower group that appeared to have two hostages. She had her left arm around the throat of one, while the other she kept at gunpoint. She was also shouting upward as though she thought someone above would hear her and give up if it saved these two's lives. Both of the hostages were men.

"Skin, can you reach the sonic blade in my pack and give it to me?"

Skin did as she was asked without question. Stacia took the knife, hefted it in her hand to make sure she had the weight right, then carefully aimed below before tossing the blade with a flick of her wrist. It wouldn't have the advantage of its vibratory function while it wasn't in her hand, but Stacia's aim was careful enough that she didn't need it. The knife spun on its way down to bury itself directly in the top of the Shellhead's skull. She dropped to the ground and then tumbled over the side of a catwalk, leaving her two hostages safely behind. The Shellheads that had been around her all looked up to see where the attack had come from.

"Why did you do that?" Stanton asked. "Now they know we're up here."

"That was just in case I can't keep my other promise to Cobble."

Many of the Shellheads shouted and pointed up to her as Stacia took her first tentative grips of the cliff face. From a distance, it had appeared relatively smooth, but now that she was right next to it, she could see that it was rough enough that she could probably make it to the top of the cliff. Or at least, she could under other circumstances. Normally, she didn't have two full-grown people strapped to her back and adding dead weight.

As she started climbing, several stone chips flew past her face from the potshots of the Shellheads below. Several hit her back, but although she felt both Skin and Stanton cower against her, neither of them screamed. That actually surprised and impressed Stacia. Neither of them was used to combat situations, especially Stanton, who was well known to do most of his activism behind a desk and in front of a camera. Maybe they were both made of sterner stuff that she had expected. That was good. It meant that maybe there really was a chance they could get off this planet after all. Considering the plan that General Borealis had set in motion required…

"Hey, Stacia?" Skin asked, interrupting Stacia's thoughts. "Didn't those other Shellheads all get the same training you did?"

"Sort of."

"Then why are you such a good shot while they all seem to be terrible?"

"Well, there's a story there." Another outcropping of rocks exploded over their heads, showering the three of them in sharp shards. "One I'll have to tell you later. Please, right now, I really need to concentrate."

About halfway up the cliff, Stanton tapped her on the back of the head. "Uh, looks like we're about to get company."

Stacia didn't dare risk turning her head to see. The higher up she got, the smoother the rock seemed to be. Finding hand and footholds was becoming more and more difficult. "What have we got?"

"I think it's the two Shellheads who ducked out the door when you started shooting," Stanton said.

"Any chance either of you two could take one of the pistols and try to scrub them off our backs?"

"I wouldn't even begin to know how to use those things," Stanton said. Skin, however, had been keeping a close watch of Stacia over the last several days. Stacia felt the woman shift around on her back until she had one of the pistols. There were two shots, followed by one fading scream.

"I got one!" Skin screeched, making Stacia wince. "I got one I got one I got one!"

"Oh God, his head," Stanton said. "It just... I think I'm going to be sick."

"Just remember that puking on me makes it harder for you to hold on," Stacia said. "Skin, good job, but try not to celebrate so much that you..."

"Oops."

"You dropped the pistol, didn't you?"

"Yes, she did," Stanton said. "The good news is that it hit the other Shellhead on the way down. She didn't fall, but she's struggling for her grip now."

Hopefully, that would buy Stacia the time she needed. They were near the top, but the only remaining handhold she could see was nearly a meter up.

"Okay, both of you two, be quiet. This is going to take some calculating."

Of course, this was punctuated by more bullets streaking past them and exploding in the rocks. Hardly the ideal situation in which to concentrate, but it wasn't anywhere near the most distracting place she'd ever found herself. That honor went to the time she had to escape an erupting volcano with a Shakespeare-quoting robot.

She took several deep breaths as her tactical implants did their work, calculating speed, force, trajectory, distance to the last handhold. A diagram appeared in her mind, showing exactly what she needed to do at what moment to move what height.

Complete with a banana for scale.

Stacia leaped up and grabbed at the handhold.

She missed by a few centimeters.

Apparently, a banana was a poor way to measure distance.

Her two passengers screamed as she hit the side of the cliff, failed to get a grip on anything, and then tumbled down the side. Her implants did their work better this time, though, forcing her to reach out and grab the remaining Shellhead before they dropped past and turned into blood smears on the ledges below. She was sure this was just a temporary measure, that the Shellhead would get ripped off the cliff and fall with them, but the Shellhead held on as Stacia got her fingers in a gap in the Shellhead's poorly attached armor.

"You bitch," the Shellhead said. "Let go of me or..."

"Climb," Stacia said in her ear. "Unless you want to get splattered like your friend."

The Shellhead paused, then said, "He wasn't my friend. Actually, he was a real dick." She climbed, although even for someone with her augmentations, the weight of three people, one in full armor, was an obvious strain. There were still a few shots from below that went wide.

"Hey, stop shooting at me!" the Shellhead called down. "I'm on your side!"

"I take it they're not your friends either?" Stacia asked.

"If they were before, they aren't now. I'm Kendara, by the way."

"Stacia. Nice to meet you."

A plasma shot hit somewhere below them.

"Idiots," Kendara said. "All of them should know there's no way to get an accurate plasma shot at this range."

"I don't know," Stacia said. "Some of those pistols looked like they might be the PQ models."

"Really? I didn't see that. I'll have to take a closer look. Assuming you don't kill me when we get to the top."

"I'm not going to make any promises just yet."

"Hey, can't blame a girl for trying."

"Seriously?" Stanton asked. "This is seriously the conversation that's happening right now?"

"You got anything better to talk about?" Kendara asked.

"How about not talking about anything and instead concentrating on not falling?"

"Okay, yeah, I see now," Kendara said.

"See what?" Stanton asked.

"Why the Lord Commander wants to shoot you."

At the top, the four people awkwardly pulled themselves up

over the ledge. There was still a great deal of shouting below, accompanied by the occasional random pot-shots, but it didn't look to Stacia like anyone else was trying to follow their insane escape route. They would have to take the long way around to get up, however far that might be.

Kendara collapsed with great heaving breaths as Stacia undid the rope that secured her passengers to her back. "What are you going to do with her now?" Stanton asked Stacia.

"The only smart thing to do would be to kill her so she doesn't muck up our escape," Stacia replied.

"No!" Skin shouted. "You can't! She helped us!"

"Only after I forced her," Stacia said. "Only after she was preparing to kill us."

"Stacia does have a point, guys," Kendara said between gasps. "That's the way of war sometimes."

"But this isn't a war," Stanton said. "There's no war within light-years of this planet."

Kendara shrugged, as if she fundamentally disagreed but didn't have the energy to argue.

"Are you actually arguing that I should shoot you?" Stacia asked Kendara.

"No, not at all. I'd like to live, thank you very much. I'm just saying that if you do, no hard feelings."

"And if I don't kill you, what will you do?"

"Try to catch my breath some more. I mean, Jesus, you are really heavy."

"You're not going to come after us?"

"Oh, I probably will. If I don't, I might as well throw myself right back off this cliff. It'll be quicker than whatever the Lord Commander will do if it looks like I just let you walk away."

Stacia raised the rope in her hands. "And what if it doesn't look like that at all?"

Kendara raised an eyebrow.

Within two minutes, Stacia had the ropes tied thoroughly around Kendara. "Too tight?" Stacia asked.

"No, just tight enough. Can't make it look like I could easily get out, can we?" She looked distant for a second, then said, "That jump you tried to make on the cliff. You should have been able to do it easily."

"You're right. I should have."

"It was the banana, wasn't it?"

"Yep. Always the banana."

"Man, if I ever get my hands on the jackass that programmed that in…"

Stacia pulled her a respectable distance from the cliff so she wouldn't somehow tumble off accidentally, while also making sure she could kick at anything that might try to come and take a bite out of her while she waited for the rest of the Shellheads to come along and find her.

"Is this often the way you do things?" Stanton asked Stacia.

"No. I like to think of my methods as flexible. Comfy, Kendara?"

"No, not comfortable at all. It's perfect. Hey, thanks for not shooting me."

"Any time. Maybe you can repay the favor sometime."

And with that, Stacia, Skin, and Stanton ran off, trying to put as much distance between them and Lexton's forces as possible.

13

THE FINE ART OF BEING AN UNRELIABLE NARRATOR

"Could someone please explain to me what exactly is going on?" Skin asked. "I'm feeling very confused at this point."

"Yeah, I can't say that I'm too clear on any of this either," Stanton said.

Stacia took a good look at their surroundings and decided that this would be a good enough place to stop for a while, rest, and explain herself. She was actually surprised that neither of her companions had pressed her for details before this. They'd been moving at their best speed for hours, heading in a direction that only Stacia knew to a target that shouldn't have existed on Leviathan. They'd kept their curiosity in check for this long. She figured it was finally time to come completely clean.

"We'll set up camp here," Stacia said. "Once we're settled for the night, I'll tell you both everything."

"Is it really wise to stop?" Stanton asked. "They could still be following us."

"Maybe," Stacia said. "I would even say probably. But we've got a big day ahead of us tomorrow, so we all need to be rested. Especially me. Kendara was right. You two aren't as light as you look."

"Actually, I think she was referring to you," Skin said.

"We'll take turns keeping watch for several hours while the other two sleep," Stacia said. "We'll get going long before dawn."

This particular camp was even more uncomfortable than the ones they'd been forced to make do with on the plains. The ground here was rocky and jagged with occasional quartz outcroppings jutting out like the planet itself was looking for an opportunity to stab someone. The landscape had turned into the most inhospitable one Stacia had seen on the planet yet, with nothing more than an occasional purple barbed plant growing from the cracks in the stone. On a couple of occasions, they had passed large crater-like structures that Stanton advised them to stay well away from. When Stacia asked him why, he replied that he had been told something carnivorous lived in the bottoms, although he hadn't had a chance to see one himself. Given what Stacia had seen of Leviathan so far, she was inclined to believe the rumor.

These details also made it less likely that they would be followed here, although Stacia assumed she couldn't count on that for too long. At this point, Lexton probably had her reputation riding on taking Stacia out. Stacia needed to be ready for any possibility.

Finally, they all sat down in a circle. Skin spoke first. "You lied to me." Stacia was surprised at the hurt accusation in her voice. She was also surprised at how much of a heel it made her feel.

"Yes, I did. I'm sorry."

"Why? Didn't you trust me?"

"I'd barely met you. I still haven't known you for more than three days."

"So you don't think I'm trustworthy?"

"It's not that. I had no idea if you might somehow have been planted with me by Lexton, or if you had some belief or value that might cause you to turn on me. You have to remember, you're an alien to me."

"And you're the mysterious alien invader to me. I thought I saw the chance in you to live differently, to not be certain that one day I would be skinned and draped over someone else. That's why I followed you, why I've been trying to help you. I thought... I thought maybe I wouldn't be so alone anymore."

"I'm sorry, Skin. I'm so, so sorry. Even with only another two days of knowing you, if I had to do it all over again, I would have told you the truth about what I was doing here from the beginning."

"You two are starting to lose me," Stanton said. "Could you maybe start from the beginning? Wherever the hell the beginning is."

Skin sat up straighter as a thought occurred to her. "All that stuff about your childhood. Was that all a lie, too?"

"No. It wasn't a lie. Everything I told you about my family and when I was a little girl is all true." Stacia paused, suddenly unable to make herself look Skin in the eye. "But there was one very important detail I changed."

"General Borealis?" Skin asked.

Stacia nodded. "I told you about the destruction of my home, and the fact that it is believed by many that it was caused either by someone's corruption or incompetence within the higher rankings of the Galactic Marines. But I know it wasn't General Borealis who was responsible. I know, because she was having dinner with us when it happened."

Stanton looked appraisingly at Stacia. "It's tough to guess your age with the armor, but I'd say you look a good five to ten years older than me. Would this have been before I was born?"

"Yes. I don't think your mother had even met your father yet. At the very least, he wasn't at dinner with us. As I'd said, all three of my parents were more or less retired at that point. General Borealis wasn't a general yet, but I remember my mothers jokingly calling her that, saying that she was trying to get their former positions. She was on a day's leave and had come to visit, but she still had her com equipment with her. That's how we heard the first news that there was an attack. Before anyone could do anything, the shells were raining down."

"My memories are a little hazy for a while after that, but I do clearly recall that she was the one who pulled me out of the building in time. She was also the one that rushed back in and tried to save my parents. She managed to get two out. Mama Linny only had minor injuries but was out cold. Mama Gertrude, however, almost died. Borealis had to make a choice between running back in one last time to try to find Papa, or quickly applying a medkit that would keep Mama Gertrude from bleeding out at her throat. I hold no grudge at all for the choice she made. For all I know, I could have lost two of my three parents that day instead of just one."

Stacia looked right at Stanton, both of them making unwavering eye contact. "And that was the moment where I decided that not only would I grow up to be a Galactic Marine, but that I would do everything in my power to one day pay your mother back for what she had done. I figured I owed her. One life saved in exchange for another."

"You never found out who was really responsible for the shelling?" Skin asked.

Stacia shook her head. "Still a mystery. In fact, there's still not any solid evidence that someone involved with the Galactic Marines was responsible. It's just a conspiracy theory, even if I've seen more than my share of evidence that corruption in our branch of the service is alive and well."

"But you still sound like a true believer," Stanton said.

"I am. I believe in the good the Galactic Marines can do. I also believe they need to be kept in check. This planet is the perfect example of what can happen when people with our augmentations are given too much power."

"But what about the things I heard from Lexton's people about you shooting my mother?" Stanton asked. "You're telling me none of that actually happened?"

"No, that happened. I shot General Borealis repeatedly. Last time I saw her, she was being dragged off to be put on life support."

Stanton blanched.

"But there's one important detail I haven't told anyone. It

didn't come up at my trial and no one witnessed it: she told me to shoot her. In fact, she gave me a direct order."

"Wait, are you trying to say that my mother ordered you to try to kill her?"

"No, I'm saying that she ordered me to shoot her. And to do a thorough job of it without actually killing her. It had to look like I'd actually wanted her dead."

"But that's crazy! Why would my mother ask anyone to do that?"

"Because, Stanton, no one is ever supposed to go down to the surface of Leviathan. Unless, of course, they're trying to make a political statement and actually crash instead."

Stanton's face went from pale to beet red.

"After your crash, the security around the planet was beefed up. You can imagine what kind of PR nightmare it was, for the son of a prominent Galactic Marine general to be making a protest at the most heavily guarded prison planet in the explored galaxy and then get stuck there. The powers that be didn't ever want a repeat of that. So trying to get someone in to rescue you the same way you got in was impossible. The only way to get someone here to help you was if a major, unforgivable crime was committed. Such as the attempted murder of a superior officer."

"She did that?" Stanton asked. "She made that kind of sacrifice for me?"

"Of course she did. You're her son. And I owed her. She's tried to tell me for years that I didn't owe her anything, but I couldn't rest until I felt I had paid her back. This whole thing was my idea. Trust me, it took a long time to convince her this was the only way."

Stanton sighed and looked down at his hands in his lap. "I didn't crash."

"I was wondering about that," Stacia said. "You're well known for your piloting skills. It never sat right with me that you would crash during what was, for you, a routine publicity opportunity."

"It wasn't a publicity opportunity! There are people on this planet who are suffering. The existence of the Skins has been speculated for years."

"Sure, by the same wacko conspiracy theorists who think the Galactic Marines are run by a group of secret lizard people from the Earth's core."

"Except this conspiracy theory turned out to be real, didn't it?" Stanton asked, pointing at Skin. Skin stared at his outstretched finger as though she wasn't sure if he was offering it to her or not.

"You're right," Stacia said quietly. "Your concerns were valid after all. But back to the crash. What happened?"

"Sabotage, as far as I can tell," Stanton said. "After the people at Roo-Soh nursed me back to health from my injuries, I went back to the wreck of my ship to try to investigate. I thought I saw evidence that a few major regulators in the engine had been removed prior to take-off. You know, from scorch marks where there shouldn't have been any scorch marks. But I could never be sure, because the Roo-Soh people had already begun to strip it for parts by then."

"Interesting," Stacia said. "Why would someone sabotage your ship?" But Stanton didn't need to answer that one. It was obvious. He had rubbed some people the wrong way with his meddling and revealing that there was anything less than perfect with the Galactic Marine's inescapable prison planet. Again, it all came back to corruption somewhere in the upper echelons.

"So does this mean you really are still a Galactic Marine after all?" Skin asked her.

"No," Stacia said quietly. "If it ever becomes public knowledge that this was all an escape attempt orchestrated by General Borealis, then she will be seen as guilty. She would probably end up down here right beside us. I really was stripped of my rank and dishonorably discharged. As much as being a Galactic Marine was part of me, it will never be a part of me again."

There was a long period of silence between all three of them before Stanton spoke again. "No offense, but so far it looks to me like your rescue plan is seriously flawed."

"How so?" Stacia asked.

"How about the fact that we're still here? A rescue would imply that we'd be able to get off Leviathan."

"Except nobody leaves Leviathan," Skin said.

"Nobody ever," Stanton agreed. "All you've managed to do by coming down here is make Lexton even more angry at me for trying to organize people against her than she was before."

"That might be true otherwise," Stacia said, allowing a twinkle to appear in her eye. "Except haven't either of you noticed that, ever since we escaped Roo-Soh, we're not exactly moving at random?"

Both of Stacia's companions sat up straighter. "So you do have something else up your sleeve?"

"I don't have sleeves," Stacia said, pointing at the armor on her arm.

"You know what I mean."

"I do. Finding you was just phase one. Phase two is to reach our spaceship."

Skin's mouth dropped open. "A spaceship? An actual, working ship?"

"No, that can't be possible," Stanton said.

"It shouldn't be, but we figured out a way."

"How? It's not like we have the materials to build one, and the security platforms wouldn't let one just land on the surface."

"Of course not. Anything that got close would be shot down with extreme prejudice. So we let them."

"Explain," Stanton demanded.

"That was the hardest part of all this to plan, even more so than shooting your mother in such a way to let her live but still make it look like I'd actually tried. About two days before I was discharged, an unidentified ship appeared in orbit. All attempts to hail it were ignored, even as it got closer. So it was shot down, obliterated, and crashed to Leviathan's surface where it exploded in a spectacular, very visible fireball."

"Okay, still not seeing where this helps us."

"The outside of the ship was shot. The outside of the ship

exploded. The reason the security platforms would never be able to identify its make and model is because all they saw was a cobbled together shell. If it looked like some kind of makeshift, pirate craft to them, that's because it essentially was. But inside, hidden from view, was the real ship, a luxury craft heavily modified just for this occasion. If everything went as it should, the real ship should still be safe and in a place far enough from any settlement that no one would have come to salvage from it."

"If," Stanton said. "There are a lot of things that could go wrong with that if."

"Yes, there are, the first being that someone else might have already found it, and the second being the possibility that the landing didn't happen the way we wanted and something got damaged. We're not going to know until we get there. And we'll get there tomorrow, at this pace."

"Not exactly the most elegant plan," Stanton said.

"We had to come up with it on the fly. Satellite scans of the surface implied that your ship was intact enough for you to have survived the crash, but any more thorough scans are blocked by the security platforms, so we had no idea how long you were going to remain in one piece."

"But… what happens to me when you leave?" Skin asked.

Stacia was surprised she even had to ask. "Skin, you're coming with us, assuming we don't die on the way out. That is, if you want to."

"I… I get to leave the planet? But nobody…"

"Nobody leaves Leviathan," Stacia said. "Yes, I know. That's the rule. But in case you haven't figured it out yet, my track record of adhering to rules is a bit spotty."

"I can go into space? I can see other worlds? I… I can live?"

"Yes. Hopefully. Again, there are a lot of things that could go wrong."

But Skin didn't seem to hear this last part. "I get to leave Leviathan!" She stood up and jumped up and down with a vigor and energy Stacia hadn't thought possible from someone so malnourished and scrawny. "I get to leave! I get to live! I get to…"

She stopped, suddenly serious. "I have no idea what I'm supposed to do out there."

Stacia smiled. "I'm sure we'll think of something."

"There's still a major problem that I see with this," Stanton said. "The security platforms aren't going to let anything launched from the surface outside of the atmosphere. We'll take off in this ship and get blown out of the sky within a minute."

"There's a plan for that, too. It'll be tricky, but we can make it work."

She gave them a rough idea of what they would do, and Stanton agreed that was risky as hell but could still work. Skin didn't seem to understand a word they said, but none of it tempered her enthusiasm. When they finally settled in for the night, Stacia took the first watch and told her companions to sleep. While she stood at the edge of the camp, however, she could hear Skin still moving around behind her even as Stanton snored lightly.

"Stacia?" Skin asked quietly.

"Yes?" Stacia didn't even turn around to see her. She had no doubt that Lexton and her people would come for them, and she had no idea when it might be. The last thing she wanted was for it to happen at the one moment when she had her back turned.

"You're serious that I can leave with you?"

"Assuming we don't all die in the attempt, yes, of course. Why would I lie to you about this?"

"You already lied to me once."

Stacia paused. "I'm sorry. Sincerely."

"I thought you were my friend."

Stacia cocked her head. She didn't usually make friends. She was all about her work, her duty. She had to admit, though, that over the last few days, she'd started to feel something for the young woman. Friendship didn't quite describe it. It was almost maternal, like she'd started to look at Skin, no matter how old she might be in reality, as a daughter in need of love and guidance. Stacia hardly thought she was the best person to provide that, but she thought she could definitely try.

"I am your friend."

Skin was quiet for a moment before saying, "I'm too excited to sleep. I want to have sex."

It took every fiber of Stacia's being not to laugh. "I already told you, I'm not interested."

"There's nothing I can do to change your mind?"

"Sorry, no."

"Are you sure? I'm really good at…"

"Skin, I'm sure."

Another pause. Then, "I'm going to have sex with Stanton, then."

"Remember what I said the other night? You ask permission first. And if he says no, then you have to take care of yourself *by* yourself. No exceptions, got it?"

"Got it." Stacia listened as she padded her way over to Stanton. Stacia turned around just long enough see the young woman kneel down over Stanton and look straight down into his sleeping face before poking him in the chest. Stanton snorted awake, then started violently as he saw the face with a lascivious look just inches away from him.

"Hi!" Skin said with comical enthusiasm. "I want to have sex with you!"

"Whuh? Uh…"

"Do you want to have sex with me?"

"I… I'm not sure…" He sat up and looked in Stacia's direction, as if he needed her permission.

"Don't look at me," Stacia said. "You're the one who gets to choose. As long as neither of you hurts the other without permission, I don't care."

"Do you have protection?" Stanton asked.

Skin cocked her head. "Stacia's standing right there. And we have guns."

"No, that's not what I…" He paused, staring at the young woman who was desperate to jump anyone's bones, probably thinking about whether or not STDs had a presence on Leviathan. Stacia turned and took up a position further from the camp to give them a little more privacy. The sounds they tried to muffle in the darkness told Stacia exactly what they both decided.

14
DADDY'S ADULT TOY

Stanton and Skin didn't get as much rest as they probably should have, although they both pulled themselves away from each other long enough to fulfill an hour each of sentry duty. In the early hours of the morning, Skin was as bright and cheerful as though she'd slept for twelve straight hours, while Stanton noticeably dragged as they all gathered their meager belongings. While Skin joyfully stripped down and cleaned the 808 and the three remaining plasma pistols (which she again had figured out how to take apart and put together with no help from Stacia), Stanton hobbled on over to Stacia and conferred with her in whispers.

"Stanton. You're looking sore this morning."

"Yeah. She's, uh, feisty."

"Sounded like it."

"So, no offense to her or anything, but do you think I'm going to need heavy doses of anti-virals and retro-biotics if we get off planet?"

"Given what I know of how she was treated before this? Let me just say this: anyone she was forced to be with before this probably didn't take a very proactive view of sexual health."

"Forced? So you mean..." He made an awkward gesture with his hands that, while it didn't actually mean anything, gave Stacia a pretty good idea of what he meant.

"A little bit of advice, Stanton. I have no idea if any of us will live past today, and even if we do I have no idea what the two of you might do after this, but just remember this. She's had a hard life, but neither is she a delicate flower. Treat her right, and treat her like a human."

"You feel responsible for her, don't you?"

"She's like a puppy that followed me home. How could I not feel responsible?"

"What about us? You and me, I mean."

"I don't follow you."

"If we live, I'll owe you my life."

"No. No more debts. I'm doing this because I felt like I owed your mother. If we get off Leviathan, everything is square between all of us."

"Come on. I'm my mother's son. Do you really think I'm not going to look for a time when I can repay you?"

Stacia smiled. "You can be annoying sometimes, Stanton, but there is no doubt that you're a Borealis."

"Um, thanks?"

By Stacia's rough calculations, they didn't have very far to walk today. She had been given rough coordinates ahead of time for Stanton's crash site, and more exact coordinates for the escape ship's resting place. But she had no idea what might lie between them. For the first several hours of the morning, the terrain remained much like they had seen before. The craters became shallower and less numerous. Stacia thought she caught a glimpse of something once near the bottom of one, something that looked like a huge pair of skeletal pincers, but they pulled back into the ground before Stacia could get any other details. Whatever the creatures were, they didn't leave the craters, and her party likewise refrained from going in.

Later in the day, though, the rocky territory began to give way once again to the grass-like vegetation they'd seen on the plains. The land here was hillier, and every so often, Stacia thought she could see tube-like pillars of dark rock rising high in the far distance, but otherwise they might as well be back on the plains. This included clear signs that a Wet Lisa or two had prowled this area at some time in the past, but the patches and paths of dead earth they left behind were already growing back over with grass. The plants grew fast around here, apparently, likely as an evolutionary trait to make up for the hardy appetite of the weird green puddles.

"We're approaching the place where the ship should be," Stacia said, "but it must not have landed exactly where it should have."

"What's that over there?" Stanton asked, pointing at a patch of land near the top of one of the hills where the grass didn't appear to be as thick as everything around it.

"Could be something," Stacia said. "Let's go take a look."

Keeping a close eye out for any fresh sign of Wet Lisas, they made their way over several smaller hills until they went up the much larger one that Stanton had indicated. It was obvious before they even reached the top that they were on the right track.

"Looks like something burned the ground here. Could be the cover explosion."

"Or it could have been a real explosion and our chance is gone," Stanton said

"Not feeling too optimistic, are you?" Stacia asked him.

"I was last night, but today I just keep thinking over and over about what they say."

All three of them said it at once in quiet, almost reverent tones. "Nobody leaves Leviathan." There wasn't much Stacia could say to refute that without lying. Still, she preferred to wait to see the status of the ship before she gave in to the planet's reputation.

They started to see debris as they got closer to the top. Skin thought that was a bad sign until Stacia pointed out that was part of the plan: the outer shell was supposed to be blown to hell, and anyone looking at it from the security platforms would assume there was nothing operable left. It was also a good sign in that so much usable scrap metal was still left sitting out unclaimed by any person or settlement. It meant that the ship had likely not been discovered and looted.

At the top, they stopped and looked down into the shallow valley beyond. Stacia had to admit that whomever General Borealis had clandestinely hired to take care of this part certainly knew what they were doing. The ship's position between hills gave it a perfect natural cover from prying eyes. There was an enormous scorch mark and debris field surrounding the ship exactly like they had expected.

Except there was also one detail they hadn't planned.

"Um, I know I've only ever seen a small handful of spaceships in my life," Skin said, "so maybe I'm wrong. But is that ship upside down?"

"Yes, that ship is most definitely upside down," Stanton sighed.

"This wasn't something I had a contingency plan for," Stacia said.

"Let's wait until we get closer," Stanton said, suddenly sounding full of a determination he hadn't shown before. "As long as everything is still in working order, I still might be able to do something about that."

"How?" Stacia asked.

"You yourself said I have somewhat of a reputation as a pilot. And I did in fact have to land a ship upside-down once. Theoretically, this should be the same thing in reverse."

"I'm not sure if it works that way," Stacia said, but she said nothing else. She and General Borealis had figured that Stanton, should Stacia be able to find him alive, would be the best person to pilot the ship off planet. Stacia herself had some minor flight training, and her tactical implants could give her some help, just enough that she could land a small ship in an emergency. But once it came to piloting ships that were lying on their backs, she was completely out of her comfort zone.

Stacia had to admonish Skin not to stop and pick at the debris as they went down the hill to the ship. The young woman wasn't used to seeing that much useful material just lying around, and the born survivor in her seemed to want to gather it all up just in case.

"But, we might need it..."

"Skin, no. Trust me."

"It could be used to make a house, or a sled to pull supplies, or..."

"Where we're going, we don't need to make that stuff ourselves out of scrap. All that stuff gets manufactured in mass quantities. You can walk into a store and walk away with a house bigger than anything you've ever seen, if you have a vehicle that can haul it."

Skin stared at her, her wide eyes showing her obvious disbelief that any such thing could possibly be true. Reluctantly, Skin put all the scrap she had gathered back on the ground.

By the time Stacia and Skin caught up to him, Stanton had already made a circuit around the whole outside of the ship at least once. "I recognize this make," he said. "A Cumbermarch H-85. Not exactly the type of ship I would have expected anyone to use for a rescue mission off one of the most dangerous planets in the galaxy."

"Why not?" Skin asked.

"It's basically a rich person's luxury cruiser. Maybe an older model that the trendiest people wouldn't be caught dead in anymore, but still reliable."

"Like I said, we didn't have much time to waste while we prepared for this," Stacia said. "We had to take whatever we could find. It was either this or something called a NewHouse N."

Stanton made a disgusted face. "A NewHouse N wouldn't have survived any of the crap this one needed to go through just to get here, let alone get off the planet. Why those two? There had to be plenty of better options."

"Because we didn't just need one. We needed two ships that were of exactly the same make." She explained why and what would be packed into the ship's hold.

"Makes sense, I guess," Stanton said.

"Getting one older ship no one would miss was easy," Stacia said. "Getting two that were exactly the same was a bit trickier given the time constraints. So, what do you think? Can you do something with this?"

"I think so. We need to get inside first before I can be one hundred percent certain."

Getting in proved to be interesting. The ship's boarding ramp could easily be opened with a code and a few hidden switches, but it opened from the bottom. Which meant they all had to climb all over it until they were on what was now the top. Stanton was able to hold his own on this climb, but Skin still needed help. As Stacia pushed her up the side, Skin pointed out the faded letters in chipped red paint that they passed. "What do those markings mean?"

Stanton turned his head sideways in an effort to read the upside down writing. Stacia, however, already knew. "It's the ship's name."

"Ships have names?" she asked. Then, with a little more anger and incredulity, "Ships have names even when I didn't have one?"

"Wait a second," Stanton said. "Am I reading this correctly, or did the chipping to the paint remove something important in the translation?"

"No, you're reading it correctly."

"Who would name their ship that?"

"You said yourself that it's an old luxury ship. It was probably originally owned by an old man in need of an ego boost."

"I can't read," Skin said. "What's the ship's name?"

"*Daddy's Adult Toy,*" Stacia responded.

"I don't get it."

"I'll explain the concept of adult toys to you later. I'm sure it's something you'll like quite a bit."

Once the hatch was open, they dropped down to the ceiling, being careful not to smash any more of the overhead lights.

"Inside looks a bit roughed up," Stanton said. "Is this the way it was when you got it, or are we seeing damage from its less than conventional landing?"

"My guess is that it's probably a little of both, but I couldn't say for sure. I was already taken away in handcuffs when this part of the plan went into effect."

Stanton stood straighter as something occurred to him. "Hey, are you going to be able to return to the Galactic Marines after this?"

Stacia just looked at him silently.

"But can't your name be cleared? Can't you explain what this was all about?"

"My trial and sentence was public knowledge. And the other thing that's public knowledge is no one gets off of Leviathan. If we do get off and anyone finds out…"

"It would be chaos for the Galactic Marine bureaucracy, wouldn't it?"

"There are probably people that would kill us rather than have it go public that their impenetrable prison isn't as perfect as they've been saying for over a hundred years, especially given the corruption within that we already suspect exists."

"Well, that's why we've got to go public, get all of this information out there…"

"We can't go public, Stanton. You, me, even Skin, once we leave, we're fugitives."

"What do you mean? Neither Skin nor I did anything wrong. I crashed here, and Skin was born here."

"It doesn't matter. Escaping from Leviathan is against the law."

"That's a stupid law!"

"Yes, it is. But according to the accepted public history, there is no such thing as an innocent person on Leviathan. They refuse to acknowledge that people like Skin exist, and last I saw, all efforts to change the law because of what happened to you are deadlocked. If I had to guess and subscribe to conspiracy theories, I'd say that the people responsible for keeping the law from getting changed are the same ones responsible for you crashing in the first place."

Stanton apparently didn't have anything else to say to that, instead going quiet as he stalked around the ship and inspected it in places that didn't seem of much consequence to Stacia. The luxury craft was designed, when it was right-side up, so that it could be flown by just one person if needed, yet had accommodations for up to six people. Any furniture in the rooms that hadn't been bolted down was of course strewn all about, but most of the nonessential pieces had been removed prior to the ship being sent here. Skin took a turn that the other two didn't and vanished for a time, although Stacia could swear that she heard the young woman crawling around in the ductwork. Stanton and Stacia finally ended up in the cockpit, where Stanton had to climb up onto the dangling pilot seat in order to inspect the controls.

"So?" Stacia asked. "Is there anything you can do?"

"Possibly. Obviously, no ship is ever designed to take off from the ground while upside down, but we lucked out. The thruster configuration on these Cumbermarch H-85s is such that I think I can do it. That's the good news."

"And is there bad news?"

"The bad news is that I don't how fast I can do this. It could take most of the day."

"I'm not sure if I'm comfortable with us eating up that much time."

"And the even worse news is that I can't guarantee that *Daddy's Adult Toy* won't get further damaged in the process. I can easily see some of the shielding panels getting damaged if I do this too fast, and possible loss of structural integrity if I do it too slow. I won't even know for sure if all that is possible until I cycle up the engines and do a diagnostic. It's less than optimal landing could have damaged something we haven't seen yet."

"How long to do that diagnostic?"

"Maybe half an hour if I ignore some of the less important systems. Like the bathrooms. I wouldn't try using them for a while anyway. Trying to take a dump while upside down is guaranteed to end in tears."

"Work on it. I'm going to see if I can find Skin, and then set up a guard perimeter to watch for anything or anyone unwelcome."

"I don't suppose there's food in here somewhere? I work better when I've got something in my mouth."

Stacia found and gave him part of an emergency ration of jerky, then took about ten minutes to search for Skin. The ship wasn't huge, yet Skin still managed to elude her. Finally, Stacia simple called into one of the ducts that she wanted Skin to help her outside. Skin's echoed reply from somewhere deep within the ship's innards was barely audible, but it did sound like maybe she agreed to be out in a few minutes.

After some thought, Stacia left the 808 and one of the pistols where Skin would be able to find them near the hatch, taking the two remaining plasma pistols and a sonic blade from the ship's supplies with her. Skin had started to show an ever so slight proficiency with the 808, and the plasma pistol could be a backup. Meanwhile, Stacia suspected plasma would be more effective against a Wet Lisa if she found one, although she hadn't actually tested that yet. If a threat came from anything else, Stacia was sure she would see it with plenty of time to warn the others.

Her tactical implants realized the flaw in this logic only as she was pulling herself up out of the reversed hatch. Which of course meant that she found herself standing on the belly of the ship with four guns pointed at her.

15

FINAL SHOWDOWNS ARE ALWAYS INEVITABLE

"Final showdowns are always inevitable," Lexton said. She had four Shellheads at strategic points on the ground below Stacia and on the hills, while Lexton herself stood on an upside down wing about twenty meters from Stacia. "I've actually had quite a few over the years, both before and after I was sentenced to Leviathan. In case you haven't guessed, I've won them all."

"Did you monologue before each time?" Stacia asked. "Because I would think that would get a bit tedious."

"You know, it really does," Lexton said. "Sometimes I wish I could just skip it, but it's kind of expected."

"So what are you expecting to happen here?" Stacia asked. "I'm already thinking that you're not going to just shoot me outright, because the smart thing would have been to do that already." She surreptitiously cast her eyes back down through the hatch for just a second as she heard something moving beneath her. Skin was there, the 808 in her hand, and she was staring up at Stacia with a look that was equal parts terror and confusion. Neither Lexton nor any of her people could see Skin from their angle, which Stacia could use to her advantage, but Stacia didn't know any way to communicate commands to the young woman without Lexton noticing.

Lexton shrugged. "Eh. I don't know. Torture maybe. Or I suppose I could torture Borealis and the Skin while you watch. But to be honest, that's getting kind of old by now."

"You could let us go. That would be a new one." Stacia moved the tip of her toe to the edge of the hatch, slowly enough that no one noticed. She wiggled the toe, hoping Skin would understand what Stacia wanted her to do.

She ran off deeper into the ship. That was not what Stacia had intended.

Yeah, if we survive today, we're going to need to work out some signals, Stacia thought.

"You know something? That *would* be a new one. I should try letting someone go sometime, just to see what it's like. But not today."

Stacia felt a vibration growing under her feet. *Oh, so that's what Skin went to do instead. I guess that'll work, too.*

She wasn't the only one who felt the thrumming beneath them. Lexton looked down at the ship. "No. There's no way. This ship can't..."

Stacia herself didn't know how Stanton had got the ship up and running so quickly, but she took advantage of the momentary distraction to make a dash for the side. She didn't get very far before the bullets started flying, but she didn't need to. The ship was already moving, rocking beneath them, and very obviously getting ready to flip with the two of them still standing on the underside. The back thrusters fired, the heat burning the side of the hill and flowing up directly into the face of one of the Shellheads. He covered his face and ducked down the other side of the hill, dropping his 808 as he rolled.

Three Shellheads left, plus Lexton, Stacia thought. Before she could do anything with that information, though, *Daddy's Adult Toy* flipped.

It was as though someone had grabbed it by one wing and flicked it with a single mighty finger. The force of the maneuver was more than Stacia had expected, and even though she thought she'd been prepared, she still found herself spinning head over heels, going so far that she was unable to get any tactical data before she hit the ground head first. Her vision flashed bright blue, not just from the force of the impact on her head but from her neural implants going into emergency shutdown mode.

Uh-oh. That wasn't good at all.

She struggled to get to her feet for a second, flicking her head violently to the side in an effort to get her implants booted up again. Stacia was so concerned with this that she almost forgot there was a huge ship spinning in the air over her head, and it was about to come down right where she was sitting. She scrambled out of the way just as one wing came down into the ground, crushing one of the Shellheads beneath it. Two down.

Daddy's Adult Toy shuddered and settled, now on its belly. Stanton hadn't had a chance to deploy the landing gear, so the main hatch in was now hidden beneath the bulk of the ship. Stacia had no way of getting in at the moment for a quick escape, and neither Stanton nor Skin could come out to help her. Stacia did a quick inventory of herself and realized that she'd lost her plasma pistols, probably when she'd been flying through the air. She could try looking for them, but it seemed most likely that they were now smashed into the dirt beneath the ship. That left her only with the sonic blade, which she thought would be enough under other circumstances. But she was dazed and without her implants. If one of the two remaining Shellheads came around the ship for her, or even Lexton herself if she hadn't been crushed right along with her lackey, then Stacia probably wouldn't survive the attack.

Sure enough, just as she thought that, first one Shellhead, then the other, came around the ship into view.

Stacia's heart sank when she saw the first one.

It leaped for joy, however, when she saw the second.

Both of them pointed their 808s at Stacia from close range. From here, there was no way they would miss her head, and even if they did, the bullets would be concentrated enough to wear down her armor rather quickly and then rip her apart. Stacia thought she heard a scream or a shout from just over the hill that was abruptly cut off, but that was not the problem immediately in front of her face.

"Hands up," the first Shellhead said.

Stacia did nothing of the sort. She didn't even look at the first. All her concentration was on the second, who had her weapon not quite trained on Stacia at all. Instead, it was pointed roughly halfway between her and the other Shellhead.

"I said hands up, or I'll blow your head off!"

Stacia again ignored him, instead speaking to the one off to his side.

"Do you remember what we said to each other on the cliff?"

The first Shellhead looked confused. He didn't even seem to understand that Stacia wasn't addressing him. "I have no idea what you're talking about."

"You said thanks for not shooting you in the head. And you remember what I said."

The first Shellhead raised his weapon. "Okay. That's enough of this. You know..."

Stacia never found out what she was supposed to know, because that was when Kendara shifted her aim and blew the Shellhead's brain clear out of his body. As bits of skull and gray matter showered down around them, Kendara lowered her weapon.

"You said maybe I could return the favor someday," Kendara said.

"So I guess that makes us even."

"Not the way I see it."

"Oh?" Stacia asked.

"The deal was that I not shoot you when I had the chance. Shooting Lucifer here, though, I figure that means you still owe me something."

"And what would that be?"

"Take me with you. I want off of this gods-forsaken hellhole of a planet."

Even though Kendara still could have shot her at any moment, Stacia hesitated. Her mission all along had been to rescue Stanton, and taking Skin was a no-brainer, considering she was an innocent that had never done anything to deserve being her. Kendara, however, was here for a reason.

"What were you sentenced to Leviathan for?" Stacia asked.

Kendara tensed before answering. "That doesn't matter."

"I think it does."

"I'm here for murder."

Before Stacia could say that no, she wouldn't take her under any circumstances, Kendara sheepishly added, "I'd take it back, if I could. A guy in a market tried to sell me something, and I just snapped. Completely lost it."

"What did he try to sell you?"

Kendara paused, then mumbled something incoherent.

"What was that?"

"A banana, all right? Some poor schmuck of a fruit salesman in the market got too aggressive in trying to sell me a banana, and I snapped, okay?"

It wasn't funny. It really wasn't. But Stacia couldn't keep a smile from her face.

"I swear," Kendara said, "if I ever get a hold of that implant programmer…"

"Drop your weapon and you can come with," Stacia said. "I can't guarantee what might and might not happen to you after we leave, but…"

Lexton jumped out from a hiding place alongside the ship and slammed Kendara in the head with both hands balled into one fist. Kendara dropped to the side, unconscious but still breathing, leaving Lexton to stand over Stacia. Lexton might not have been armed while Stacia was, but Lexton's implants were probably still working. That made the two of them about evenly matched.

That wasn't good enough for Stacia.

"You know, after careful consideration, I have definitely decided not to let you go," Lexton said. Stacia barely listened. Instead, she looked up to the top of the hill where the Shellhead had vanished when the engines started. Now that she thought about it, that was the direction that random scream had come from.

Just over the edge of the hill, several stalks of grass

disappeared from view.

"Okay then," Stacia said as she stood up. "Let's finish this."

Lexton took a defensive stance, ready to defend herself against Stacia's initial attack. Stacia rushed, but instead of going right toward Lexton with her knife, she dashed around the confused woman and ran up the hill.

"Wha... You're not supposed to run!" Lexton called after her. "That's not how these things work!" Then, in a quieter voice as she gave chase, "Damn it."

Stacia didn't go far. She stopped just short of the top of the hill, where she saw more grass vanishing. She didn't want Lexton to see that, though. If she even so much as glanced in that direction, her tactical implants, as old as they were, would still pick it up and alert her to what Stacia had planned. So instead, Stacia lunged at Lexton, knife aimed right for the woman's throat. Lexton parried the attack easily, and without the benefit of her implants, Stacia couldn't quite make the next decision quick enough to avoid Lexton grabbing her by the wrist. They locked in an embrace as Stacia tried to get the sonic blade close enough to stab Lexton, while Lexton did her best to twist Stacia's wrist and turn the blade back on its owner.

"Your implants are malfunctioning, aren't they?" Lexton asked. "You want to know something? They always do, at some point. That's why I always win. Because eventually, whoever I'm up against, they reach this point and don't know what to do. It's a crutch that I don't have."

Stacia, straining against Lexton's strength, couldn't help smiling through her grimace. "You don't have tactical neural implants?"

"Mine permanently failed long ago. I don't need them."

"That's actually good to know. It means you can't predict when I do *this*!"

Stacia used Lexton's own strength against her, letting the sonic blade come down to nick her own armor but using the momentum to throw them both off balance. They hit the ground, and Stacia felt the sonic blade slice through her armor and into her abdomen. Lexton was so surprised by the maneuver that she let go as Stacia rolled the two of them over the edge of the hill.

And right into the Wet Lisa that had been waiting on the other side.

They both splashed into the slimy green puddle, but Lexton's removable armor proved less capable of preventing the ooze from getting in the cracks of the armor's plates. Lexton screamed as the tender flesh in her joints dissolved in the Wet Lisa's acid, but she regained control long enough to keep rolling until she was on top and Stacia was beneath her. Stacia held her head up, keeping it from falling back into the slime, but she was sure her hair was dissolving as it hung in the goop.

"This was your plan?" Lexton asked as she held Stacia down, trying to shove her head back into the Wet Lisa. "It doesn't seem to be working out very well for you."

"Actually, I just needed to get you into a good position to do this." She yanked her head to the side, again letting Lexton's own force work against her as her hand slipped from Stacia's face and plunged right into the Wet Lisa. Her glove kept most of the corrosive substance out, but the sudden shift allowed Stacia to get out from under her, grab the woman by the back of her head, and shove with all her might.

Half of Lexton's face, the side that hadn't long ago been a Wet Lisa's meal, plunged right into the creature. Lexton didn't even get a chance to scream as the right side of her face became a sizzling ruin to match the left.

16
NO ONE LEAVES LEVIATHAN

Stacia left Lexton's body to the Wet Lisa and made her way back down the hill, this time significantly slower than when she had gone up. When she pulled the sonic blade out of her gut, her armor automatically filled the wound with healing foam that would both help to mend the flesh and keep her from bleeding out. That didn't mean the stab wound didn't hurt like all hell, and Stacia doubted that she would be in any condition to fight anymore. Theoretically, she wouldn't have to. All that remained was getting off Leviathan, and that would all be up to Stanton.

Daddy's Adult Toy started to rise on its landing gear as Stacia got to the bottom of the hill. Kendara was likewise getting up, although she looked shaky. "Please tell me she's dead," she said.

"A Wet Lisa is finishing her off as we speak," Stacia said. She helped Kendara steady herself, although it might have been more accurate to say that they had to steady each other. Once the landing gear finished deploying, the hatch, which had slammed shut when the ship did it acrobatics, opened up as well. The mechanisms didn't sound like they were entirely in working order, and the ramp stopped just short of the ground. As long as it would close when they needed it to, though, that was all that mattered.

Stacia stopped and hung her head.

"What's wrong?" Kendara asked.

"My implants are rebooting. I keep seeing that little spinning circle. It's making me dizzy."

"Maybe you should sit down and…"

Gunfire erupted from behind them, and they both dropped to the ground. Stacia turned to look and saw Lexton, or at least Lexton from the neck down. Her face was completely gone, leaving only a dripping mess of gore behind.

"I thought you said she was dead!" Kendara said.

"I said she was being eaten! Not the same thing!"

"Really? You're arguing semantics now?"

It sounded like Lexton was trying to say something, but there wasn't enough of her mouth or tongue for it to be anything other than a guttural, angry roar. She'd must have stumbled on one of the dropped 808s and was firing blindly around her, aware that if she kept shooting for long enough she would inevitably hit someone or something important, getting at least a small measure of revenge before she died.

Another burst of 808 fires came from nearby. Most of the shots missed, but enough found their mark that Lexton finally toppled over dead, a few last rounds emitting from her 808 before it stopped.

Stacia looked back to the hatch to see Skin crouching on the partially lowered gangway, the 808 Stacia had left for her in the young woman's hand. Skin looked with disbelief, first at her weapon, then at Lexton's corpse, then at Stacia.

"I didn't drop it this time," Skin said in a reverent whisper.

Stacia stood back up, both using Kendara for support and helping her up at the same time. "Very nice. We might make a Galactic Marine out of you yet."

Skin's face fell. "Please don't. I like my skin."

Stacia hobbled over and gently put a hand on Skin's arm. "I'm sorry. That was thoughtless of me. I didn't mean it like that."

Skin nodded, although she still looked skittish as the idea that the two former Galactic Marines in front of her might still flay her yet. Stacia and Kendara both climbed up into the hatch and then closed it before making their way to the cockpit, where they found Stanton sitting at the controls with a notably grim expression.

"Thanks," Stacia said to him. "I'm pretty sure that saved my life."

"Don't go thanking me yet," Stanton said. He paused to look at Kendara, then shrugged when this apparently didn't surprise him that much. "I'm not sure at this point that we're going to survive the rest of the day."

"I take it that little maneuver of yours didn't agree with the ship?" Stacia asked.

"Nope. Not at all."

"How long would it take for us to make repairs?"

"A couple of weeks."

"You've probably got less than an hour," Kendara said. "Lexton had backup on the way. She jumped the gun in coming after you. I guess you must have pissed her off more than most people."

"Can't we just shoot them again?" Skin asked.

"I'm not in any condition to do any more fighting," Stacia said. "I know I tend to make it look easy, but even I have my limits."

"And there's at least six in the group that's coming," Kendara said. "Maybe more, for all I know."

"So we probably need to be off the ground and in the air by then," Stacia said.

"Is the ship at least healthy enough that we can fly it to another location long enough to make all the needed repairs?" Kendara asked.

"No. If anything launches from the surface at all, the security platforms in orbit will shoot it down within minutes," Stacia said. "We're lucky they didn't register the ship flipping as it taking off, or else we would already be slag. Once the ship takes off, it's outer space or bust. We can only try the escape plan once."

"So you guys actually have one?" Kendara asked. "Care to clue me in?"

"Does it really matter? If it works, you're free, and if it

doesn't, you're bloody shrapnel."

"True enough, I suppose."

Stacia indicated Kendara and Skin. "You two go find a seat and strap yourselves in tight. There's nothing else you can do now." She looked at Stanton. "Unless you think there's something one of them can repair in the short time we have left?"

"If they want to do everything they can to make sure the hatch is sealed, there's that. Other than that, there's no time for anything else."

The two of them went, leaving Stacia to strap into the seat next to Stanton. "Give it to me straight," she said. "Just how screwed are we really?"

"You really want to know?"

"Yes."

"If we take off now, I see no way we make it into orbit. That little stunt I pulled forced me to cold-start the reactors, which they're not designed to do. I didn't even get anywhere near a full diagnostic, so I have no idea what damage might have been done during the *Toy*'s original landing. And then you add to the mix any damage done when it hit the ground after the flip."

"So you're saying the number of things that could and should be wrong with the ship are numerous, but you don't actually know for sure about any of it?"

"Like I said, no time for the diagnostics. I could start running them now and they might be finished by the time we get attacked the rest of Lexton's people."

"And repairs? Is there any time for anything at all?"

"Maybe a few smalls ones. Which, again, we don't even know what they are yet."

Stacia shook her head, less at the situation than in an attempt to get her implants to reboot faster. They were pretty much like the ship at this point: she had no idea what might be wrong with them, and had no time to do anything about it. She would have to make this decision without their help.

No cybernetic implants, no energy to physically fight, she thought. *This is where we put my Galactic Marine training to the real test.*

"Okay," Stacia said. "Take off."

"Seriously?"

"Dead serious. According to you, there's not much we can do to repair anything. So there's no point in putting this off. We do this now, before we all lose our nerve."

"But we're all going to die!"

"Isn't that kind of the point?"

Stanton looked like he was about to ask what that was supposed to mean, but he stopped as a look of grim understanding came over his face. "Are you ready to die?"

"I guess I am," Stacia said. "You?"

"Hell no. But since when has death waited for people to be ready?"

He flicked a number of switches, and the engines, which had been in stand-by mode, roared to full power. He made a quick announcement over the intercom that Skin and Kendara had better be strapped in, then he pushed forward the lever that brought *Daddy's Adult Toy* into the air.

"Do you remember the coordinates I gave you last night while we were talking about this?" Stacia asked.

"Yep. Looks like they're just over a kilometer from here."

"Stay under fifty meters until we get to that point. The security platforms shouldn't pick us up until then."

"That's going to be difficult with these hills."

"I guess that means now's your chance to prove that your crash wasn't really your fault."

A startling number of red lights and alarms went off as Stanton skimmed the hilly surface on the way to their final launch point. Stanton gave most of the lights no more than a cursory glance before he shut them off, but a couple he left on even though he quieted their alarms. Stacia raised an eyebrow at this, but Stanton either didn't notice or else couldn't be bothered to answer her silent question. Apparently, he was in the zone, which was exactly where Stacia needed him to stay.

Just before they reached the coordinates, Stacia saw a number of Shellheads coming over a distant hill. Whether Kendara had lied or simply been wrong, there were significantly more than she had said. If they had waited, they would have been slaughtered. It seemed that Stacia had made the right decision in taking off right away, or at least the decision that was less wrong.

"Okay," Stanton said. "We're at the coordinates without getting blown out of the sky yet. Want to double check to make sure I've got them right?"

"Look's correct."

"And what exactly is it supposed to do if we fly up from here?"

"The security platforms in orbit are positioned so that up to five of them can fire on one location all at once for maximum likelihood of hitting their target even from orbit. When we were planning this, however, we found a few spots where the system isn't quite as secure. If we start up from here, we'll have only two of the platforms targeting us to start with, and only one able to get us after we leave the atmosphere. Do you remember what you're supposed to do at the end?"

"I do, but again, I can't be sure the ship is in any shape to do it."

"Too late to worry about that now. Any last words?"

"How about 'Nobody leaves Leviathan?'"

"Nobody but us," Stacia said. "Hit it."

Stanton pulled back on the stick, engaged the thrusters, and shot *Daddy's Adult Toy* straight up into the air. Stacia had approximately one to two minutes to contemplate the way the g-forces felt like they were trying to rip her apart before they were likely to encounter the first salvo from orbit. Normally, a ship leaving a planet didn't have to go this fast anymore, or at this extreme of an angle. Even so, the inertial dampeners should have been limiting the gravitational effects of the takeoff on them. Apparently, that had been one of the flashing red lights. From somewhere behind Stacia in the ship (or beneath her, depending on how she looked at it), Skin screamed at the sudden shock to her system. Stacia felt a sudden swell of pity for the young woman.

She'd never even seen a ship take off from the planet's surface, let alone been in one, and she would be completely unprepared for the roughness of their trip. With any luck, Stacia would be able to comfort her later. For now, trying to get out of her seat to go back to her would be suicide.

Another warning went off on the console, this time one Stacia clearly recognized. "First energy salvo from the platforms coming toward us."

"I see that on the instruments," Stanton said. "Hold on."

"I'm already holding on!"

"Well, hold on harder."

Stanton pulled the stick in a quick jerk to the left. Somehow, the gravitational forces pulling at her managed to get worse for a moment, and the entire ship shimmied to the side just in time to miss an enormous beam of energy lancing down at them. It vanished out of view below, no doubt hitting somewhere in the hills and vaporizing everything unlucky enough to be in its path.

"I think that one might have singed a wing," Stanton said through gritted teeth.

"The other platform just fired off two beams at once."

"Crap. This one's going to be tricky." Stanton pulled back on the stick so far that they were practically upside down compared to the ground. Stacia couldn't see the beams from this angle, but the instruments showed that they criss-crossed right where the *Toy* would have been if not for Stanton's maneuver. As Stanton wrestled with the stick in an effort to bring the ship back on the right course, the entire craft started to rattle and shake.

"I'm assuming it's not supposed to do that?" Stacia asked.

"No. That's bad."

"Can the platforms see that we're having problems?"

"Most likely."

"Okay. Time to do it then."

"No, we need to wait until we're higher."

"If I say it's time…"

"You may be the rescuer, but I'm the pilot, and I say that if we try your final trick before we reach vacuum, then we're all going back down to Leviathan the hard way."

Stacia would have nodded if her head wasn't plastered against the back of her seat. "Okay. I trust you."

"You might want to have the switch for the hold doors ready, though. Our window of opportunity is going to be small."

Two more beams shot past them, both of which Stanton was able to dodge, but with every maneuver, the ship's shimmy got worse. A large number of new red lights lit up all across the control panels, including one very large and ominous one that Stacia recognized as belonging to the reactor.

"Stanton..."

"I see that, too. Can't do anything about it."

I gave up being a Galactic Marine for this, Stacia thought. *Everything that ever meant anything to me. Was it worth it?* She looked over at Stanton, the son of the woman who had saved her family. One way or the other, Stacia's part in all this was done. She'd fulfilled the vow she'd made before she'd even been old enough to truly know what a vow was.

Yes. It was worth it.

"They're changing tactics," Stacia said. "Instruments show them launching a barrage of missiles."

"How many?"

"Uh, all of them, it looks like. Every missile ever. How much longer until we're in position?"

"Thirty seconds."

Stacia didn't bother to tell him what he likely already knew. Missiles would not be as fast as the plasma beams, but that kind of wall of explosive material would be near impossible to dodge. And the instruments said they would strike in twenty-six seconds.

In a last moment of inspiration, Stacia opened a channel to the platforms, then talked as though she'd just done it by accident. "We're not going to make it!"

"We can make it. Just make sure you..." Stacia almost turned off the channel, but he seemed to understand what she was doing just before he gave their plan away. "Just keep hanging on!"

Nineteen seconds. Stacia forced a hand onto the lever that

would blow the emergency explosives on the cargo hold doors.

"I can't do it!" Stanton said. "I can't dodge them!" Despite his words, he gripped the stick tighter.

Fifteen seconds.

Stacia had a sudden moment of mischievous inspiration. "Mamas, I love you both."

Ten seconds.

Something very violently shuddered from the back of the ship. Skin screamed again, this time accompanied by Kendara. Stacia hoped the com channel picked that up, then switched it off abruptly.

Seven seconds.

Stanton quickly glanced to make sure that the channel was off, then said, "Stacia, get ready…"

Four seconds.

Stanton yanked on the stick hard.

Two seconds.

Stacia blew the cargo hold doors.

Zero.

The air filled with a spectacular explosion. For several seconds, no one monitoring the ship from the security platforms could see anything.

But when the flash cleared and they zoomed in on what little of the debris hadn't been vaporized, they could clearly see the charred words *Daddy's Adult Toy* on a fragment of the ship tumbling back to Leviathan.

The security teams all cheered, not knowing yet that they were about to be the center of one of the biggest political firestorms in Galactic Marines history. They celebrated because, although it had been a close call, they had still proven that old maxim to be true.

Nobody left Leviathan. Not alive, at least.

17
THEN THEY ALL DIED, THE END

"Good day or good evening, wherever you might be. I'm Lawrence Zawayon. Our top story today, the fallout from the recent revelations surrounding the planet Leviathan continues. The rumors have been confirmed that Stanton Borealis, notable activist and son of a prominent general in the Galactic Marines, was indeed aboard the ship that recently tried to leave the planet. QLN News Node has acquired the video that he managed to broadcast before his attempt to leave..."

"I doubt that I'm going to survive this, which is why I'm making sure this message is released prior to our taking off. I just hope that it reaches someone outside the military. I have not been allowed to leave, despite the continued assertions we have all heard from Galactic Marine command that Leviathan is not a prison planet. I can also confirm that all the rumors are true. There are, in fact, people living here, people born here, that were not convicted of any crimes. There are rampant and unbelievable sentient rights abuses, including..."

"The rest of the video goes into graphic details. For those who wish to see it all, the rest is available at our sister news node, AQV. While no official statement has yet been released by the Galactic Marines, one source we found that wishes to remain anonymous insists that the video, along with the woman who appears in it later claiming to be one of the native-born of Leviathan, are elaborate hoaxes. While Borealis's mother, the General Lita Borealis, is still in recovery from wounds she received in an unrelated attack, she did release this statement: 'I continue to support the mission of the Galactic Marines and always will. But someone within command must be held accountable for the senseless murder of my son, and teams must be sent to Leviathan to judge the legitimacy of his claims.' Public outcry is growing, with a vocal contingent calling for the Planetary Congress to begin an official investigation. In other news, rogue forces on the planet Behemoth continue their coup, with their leader…"

Stacia turned off the holofeed. Kendara gave a feeble protest that she had been watching that, then nodded off and proceeded to snore as the pain medications coursing through her system took effect. All four of them were sharing the same room together, an anti-septically white medical room with harsh lighting that made it hard for any of them to sleep without the benefit of medications. Less than perfect as it was, though, it was still better than being ripped-apart atoms floating in orbit around Leviathan.

Their escape had been closer than Stacia had wanted, and Kendara had even come close to not making it. Stanton's maneuver had blown out the last of the inertial dampeners, resulting in all of them receiving some variety of broken bones and damaged organs from their final jump out of the system, which in itself had already been more dangerous thanks to their close proximity to Leviathan's gravity well. Stacia's blowing of the cargo doors had also exposed a flaw in the integrity of the hold itself, meaning that when they had vented the pieces of *Daddy's Adult Toy*'s exact duplicate into space, several areas of the ship had suffered dangerous levels of decompression. Multiple pieces of shrapnel from the exploding decoy parts as they hit the missiles had damaged their engines on the way out. This, along with the fact that their reactors had already been failing, meant that the ship had stopped before its planned rendezvous point and floated in the void, slowly venting their precious air, for over an hour before their rescuers had finally traced their route and found them. Life support systems would have held out for another hour or two at most, and they all would have died if there hadn't already been a small group of people expecting them.

But instead of dying, they'd "died."

Stanton had suffered the fewest injuries when they'd faked their death, which was good because they'd needed him to film the video they had leaked to the press soon after. No one watching it from the comforts of their own home would be any wiser that half the cuts and bruises on his face hadn't been obtained on the planet at all. Skin's part in the video had been a little shakier, since she'd never had to act in front of a camera before, and she was still recovering from the shock to her system that was her first space flight. It hadn't been so much of a shock, though, that she hadn't later snuck into Stanton's bed several times when she thought Kendara and Stacia were asleep.

So that was it. To the rest of the galaxy, they were all dead, and their final moments had been used to expose just how bad things were on Leviathan. The mission was done. Stacia had rescued her charge, along with two extras just for good measure. If it had been any other mission, Stacia would have been satisfied and ready for a rest before getting back to battle.

Except there wouldn't be any more battles, no more missions. She wasn't a Galactic Marine anymore, and never could be again. The entire point of her life, even the debt she had sworn to repay when she was a child, was now over and done with.

All she had now was her beat-up, secondhand armor and a hospital bed. She would be lying if she said that she hadn't considered several times just going to the nearest airlock and spacing herself.

The light over their door turned from red to green, indicating that they were about to get a visitor. Security was understandably tight, considering they were all supposed to be dead. If the wrong people found out they were still alive (and they still weren't even positive who these wrong people might be), there would be hell to pay. Once the unsavory elements were rooted out of the Galactic

Marine High Command, then maybe they could come forth and tell everyone they were still alive. Until then, though, the number of people allowed into this room were two doctors, two nurses, and anyone else General Borealis still trusted.

Figuring their visitor had to be a doctor or nurse, Stacia sat up in her bed, wincing at the pain from the wound mending under her armor. She didn't want any of the medical staff to see her looking weak, as futile as that might sound to anyone else.

It wasn't a doctor or nurse, though. When the door opened, Mama Gertrude and Mama Linny walked in.

Stacia scrambled out of her bed, ignoring the pain, and found herself torn between standing at attention to salute them and running to hug them. Her mothers made the decision for her when they both opened their arms wide, so Stacia ran to embrace them.

"I did it, Mamas," Stacia whispered.

"We know you did, honey," Mama Gertrude said. "We never doubted for a moment that you would."

Stacia backed away, falling back on her military training and standing at attention. Mama Linny appeared amused by this, while Mama Gertrude looked sad. For a moment, Stacia couldn't figure out why. Then she remembered.

She wasn't a Galactic Marine anymore. They were no longer her superior officers.

"What are you two doing here?" Stacia asked. "This place is supposed to be on a need-to-know basis only."

"That's why we don't actually even know where here is," Mama Linny said. "A friend brought us along, but we had to be kept in isolation the entire time so we wouldn't have a clue as to the coordinates."

"A friend?" Stacia asked.

The two of them stepped to either side, allowing General Borealis to come in from behind them.

This time, Stacia didn't care whether she was still a Galactic Marine or not. She saluted anyway.

"General! I wasn't expecting you just yet."

"At ease, marine," Borealis said. Her voice was shaky, and

despite the brand new Scorpio-class armor she was wearing, the woman still had to walk with a cane. Borealis saw Stacia staring at it and chuckled.

"Next time I give you an order to shoot me, marine, maybe you could not be so thorough, huh?"

"Sorry, General."

"Don't be too sorry. It convinced all the right people, didn't it? No one ever suspected a thing."

"Is the damage permanent?"

"Once upon a time, it might have been. You hit a few key nerves. But with the right therapy, I should be back to normal within six months."

"To what do we owe the pleasure of your presence?"

"Well, for one thing, I came to see my son." General Borealis came further into the room and stood next to Stanton's bed. "I don't want to disturb him, though. Any idea when he might be waking up?"

"In complete honesty, general, given his recent activities with Skin this morning, I expect he's really going to need a lot more rest."

"Ha! I suppose." Careful not to wake him, General Borealis brushed a stray strand of hair off his forehead and, after a moment's hesitation, bent down to gently kiss her son's cheek. When she stood back up, she went over to Skin's bedside. "Skin, huh? That's the best name you could give her?"

"It's the name she wanted."

"And everything she said in the video is true? Do the convicts really use people like her for..." The general, veteran of more bloody conflicts than most marines saw in their entire lifetimes, couldn't even bring herself to continue that sentence.

"I saw more than enough evidence to corroborate her tale."

"This will start to change now, you know," General Borealis said. "Her claims will be investigated. The Skins will be freed from that living hell."

"Eventually," Stacia said.

"Yes," the general said with a sigh. "Eventually. It does seem that none of the important stuff can ever be done quickly, can it? There are always rules. Red tape. People trying to obstruct the truth." She turned to Stacia with a distinct gleam in her eye. "How would you like to do something about that?"

"General? I don't understand."

"She was telling us her plan on the way here," Mama Gertrude said.

Mama Linny nodded. "And we both agreed that if there was anyone who would want to be involved, it was you."

"I don't understand," Stacia said.

"Leviathan is only one planet, Stacia. The vast majority of the planets we have found and colonized, or at least established relationships with, are stable and just in their own way. On a few, when something goes wrong, the Galactic Marines can go in. But on fewer still, the brute force of the Galactic Marines isn't the answer. In fact, as I'm sure you saw down on Leviathan, the marines are actually the problem. There needs to be some sort of last line, a group of people who can go in without anyone suspecting, to do what's right."

"And who determines what's right and what's not?" Stacia asked.

"Who indeed? Maybe there needs to be certain people involved. Like a person with a strong sense of duty and justice." She put a hand on Stacia's shoulder, then looked at Stanton. "And someone with pure intentions and a strong belief in what's right and wrong." She nodded to Skin. "Someone who has lived through the worst of what sentient beings can do to each other, and will have empathy for the oppressed." And then she shrugged at Kendara. "And perhaps even a wildcard. Someone who isn't so pure. Just in case there's something unsavory that must be done that the pure cannot."

"Us?" Stacia asked. "You want us to be this team of yours."

"You would be top secret. You would answer only to me and a small number of others that I deem trustworthy."

"That would be us," Mama Linny said.

"There's still plenty that's fishy going on in the Galactic

Marine command. Stanton's ship didn't go down all by itself, and there are other things I've witnessed. I don't have much to go on yet, but I get the feeling that someone will need to stand up to whatever corruption is growing inside the Galactic Marines. You may not technically be a marine anymore, but you can still serve. You can still do what's right. Hell, you even already have a ship to use, once it's fixed. Although I suggest maybe changing the name."

Stacia smiled. "I don't know. No would expect the secret team of a Galactic Marines general to tool around the galaxy in a ship called *Daddy's Adult Toy*. It might be the perfect camouflage."

Borealis smiled back. "Maybe it might be. So what do you say? Is this a call you think you might want to answer?"

Stacia considered it for all of three seconds. Then the smile disappeared from her face, she stood at attention again, and she gave her best Galactic Marine salute.

"Stacia X-79, reporting for duty, General."

THE END

 SEVERED**PRESS**

facebook.com/severedpress
twitter.com/severedpress

CHECK OUT OTHER GREAT SCIENCE FICTION BOOKS

SALVAGE MERC ONE
by Jake Bible

Joseph Laribeau was born to be a Marine in the Galactic Fleet. He was born to fight the alien enemies known as the Skrang Alliance and travel the galaxy doing his duty as a Marine Sergeant. But when the War ended and Joe found himself medically discharged, the best job ever was over and he never thought he'd find his way again.

Then a beautiful alien walked into his life and offered him a chance at something even greater than the Fleet, a chance to serve with the Salvage Merc Corp.

Now known as Salvage Merc One Eighty-Four, Joe Laribeau is given the ultimate assignment by the SMC bosses. To his surprise it is neither a military nor a corporate salvage. Rather, Joe has to risk his life for one of his own. He has to find and bring back the legend that started the Corp.

SERENGETI
by J.B. Rockwell

It was supposed to be an easy job: find the Dark Star Revolution Starships, destroy them, and go home. But a booby-trapped vessel decimates the Meridian Alliance fleet, leaving Serengeti—a Valkyrie class warship with a sentient AI brain—on her own; wrecked and abandoned in an empty expanse of space. On the edge of total failure, Serengeti thinks only of her crew. She herds the survivors into a lifeboat, intending to sling them into space. But the escape pod sticks in her belly, locking the cryogenically frozen crew inside.

Then a scavenger ship arrives to pick Serengeti's bones clean. Her engines dead, her guns long silenced, Serengeti and her last two robots must find a way to fight the scavengers off and save the crew trapped inside her.

 SEVEREDPRESS

facebook.com/severedpress
twitter.com/severedpress

CHECK OUT OTHER GREAT SCIENCE FICTION BOOKS

MAUSOLEUM 2069
by Rick Jones

Political dignitaries including the President of the Federation gather for a ceremony onboard Mausoleum 2069. But when a cloud of interstellar dust passes through the galaxy and eclipses Earth, the tenants within the walls of Mausoleum 2069 are reborn and the undead begin to rise. As the struggle between life and death onboard the mausoleum develops, Eriq Wyman, a one-time member of a Special ops team called the Force Elite, is given the task to lead the President to the safety of Earth. But is Earth like Mausoleum 2069? A landscape of the living dead? Has the war of the Apocalypse finally begun? With so many questions there is only one certainty: in space there is nowhere to run and nowhere to hide.

RED CARBON
by D.J. Goodman

Diamonds have been discovered on Mars.

After years of neglect to space programs around the world, a ruthless corporation has made it to the Red Planet first, establishing their own mining operation with its own rules and laws, its own class system, and little oversight from Earth. Conditions are harsh, but its people have learned how to make the Martian colony home.

But something has gone catastrophically wrong on Earth. As the colony leaders try to cover it up, hacker Leah Hartnup is getting suspicious. Her boundless curiosity will lead her to a horrifying truth: they are cut off, possibly forever. There are no more supplies coming. There will be no more support. There is no more mission to accomplish. All that's left is one goal: survival.

SEVERED**PRESS**

f facebook.com/severedpress
twitter.com/severedpress

CHECK OUT OTHER GREAT SCIENCE FICTION BOOKS

IN PERPETUITY
by Jake Bible

For two thousand years, Earth and her many colonies across the galaxy have fought against the Estelian menace. Having faced overwhelming losses, the CSC has instituted the largest military draft ever, conscripting millions into the battle against the aliens. Major Bartram North has been tasked with the unenviable task of coordinating the military education of hundreds of thousands of recruits and turning them into troops ready to fight and die for the cause.

As Major North struggles to maintain a training pace that the CSC insists upon, he realizes something isn't right on the Perpetuity. But before he can investigate, the station dissolves into madness brought on by the physical booster known as pharma. Unfortunately for Major North, that is not the only nightmare he faces- an armada of Estelian warships is on the edge of the solar system and headed right for Earth!

BATTLEFIELD MARS
by David Robbins

Several centuries into the future, Earth has established three colonies on Mars. No indigenous life has been discovered, and humankind looks forward to making the Red Planet their own.

Then 'something' emerges out of a long-extinct volcano and doesn't like what the humans are doing.

Captain Archard Rahn, United Nations Interplanetary Corps, tries to stem the rising tide of slaughter. But the Martians are more than they seem, and it isn't long before Mars erupts in all-out war.

SEVEREDPRESS

 facebook.com/severedpress
 twitter.com/severedpress

CHECK OUT OTHER GREAT SCIENCE FICTION BOOKS

FURNACE
by Joseph Williams

On a routine escort mission to a human colony, Lieutenant Michael Chalmers is pulled out of hyper-sleep a month early. The RSA Rockne Hummel is well off course and—as the ship's navigator—it's up to him to figure out why. It's supposed to be a simple fix, but when he attempts to identify their position in the known universe, nothing registers on his scans. The vessel has catapulted beyond the reach of starlight by at least a hundred trillion light-years. Then a planetary-mass object materializes behind them. It's burning brightly even without a star to heat it. Hundreds of damaged ships are locked in its orbit. The crew discovers there are no life-signs aboard any of them. As system failures sweep through the Hummel, neither Chalmers nor the pilot can prevent the vessel from crashing into the surface near a mysterious ancient city. And that's where the real nightmare begins.

LUNA
by Rick Chesler

On the threshold of opening the moon to tourist excursions, a private space firm owned by a visionary billionaire takes a team of non-astronauts to the lunar surface. To address concerns that the moon's barren rock may not hold long-term allure for an uber-wealthy clientele, the company's charismatic owner reveals to the group the ultimate discovery: life on the moon.

But what is initially a triumphant and world-changing moment soon gives way to unrelenting terror as the team experiences firsthand that despite their technological prowess, the moon still holds many secrets.

www.ingramcontent.com/pod-product-compliance
Lightning Source LLC
Chambersburg PA
CBHW051955170626
46808CB00007B/2639